# BE GOOD

# BE GOOD

**A 20th-century Historical Action Adventure**

Danie Botha

www.daniebotha.com

Published in the United States by Charbellini Press

ISBN  978-0-9951748-2-5 (paperback)
ISBN  978-0-9951748-3-2
ISBN: 0995174822

# Author's Note:

The Afrikaner *Broederbond* (also known as the Afrikaner Brotherhood, or AB) was founded in 1918 in South Africa, born out of the conviction that "the Afrikaner-volk was planted in the country by the hand of God." This followed sixteen years after the Second Boer War (1899-1902), when Britain conquered the two Boer Republics. In spite of the reconciliation between the British and the Afrikaners in 1910, many Boers remembered the extremely brutal tactics used by the British.

The British Federation of Rhodesia and Nyasaland was created in 1953, consisting of Southern Rhodesia, Northern Rhodesia, and Nyasaland. Those territories are now the countries of Zimbabwe, Zambia, and Malawi, respectively. The years leading up to Zambia's independence were marked by a growing awareness of African Nationalism, which led to nonviolent resistance against British colonial rule.

This Federation was dissolved on December 31, 1963. Zambia declared independence from the United Kingdom on October 24, 1964.

Scores of South African missionaries, many sent out by the Dutch Reformed Church (DRC), worked on Mission stations throughout Southern Africa during the first two-thirds of the twentieth century.

The Broederbond, with its powerful political connections, pushed the concept of separate development and Afrikaner nationalism. The AB was sympathetic to the DRC, although it denied that it ever interfered with the internal affairs of the Afrikaans churches.

*Be Good* is a work of fiction. Apart from well-known actual people, organizations, events and locales, all names, characters, and incidents are the product of the author's imagination. Any resemblance to actual persons, living or dead, is entirely coincidental.

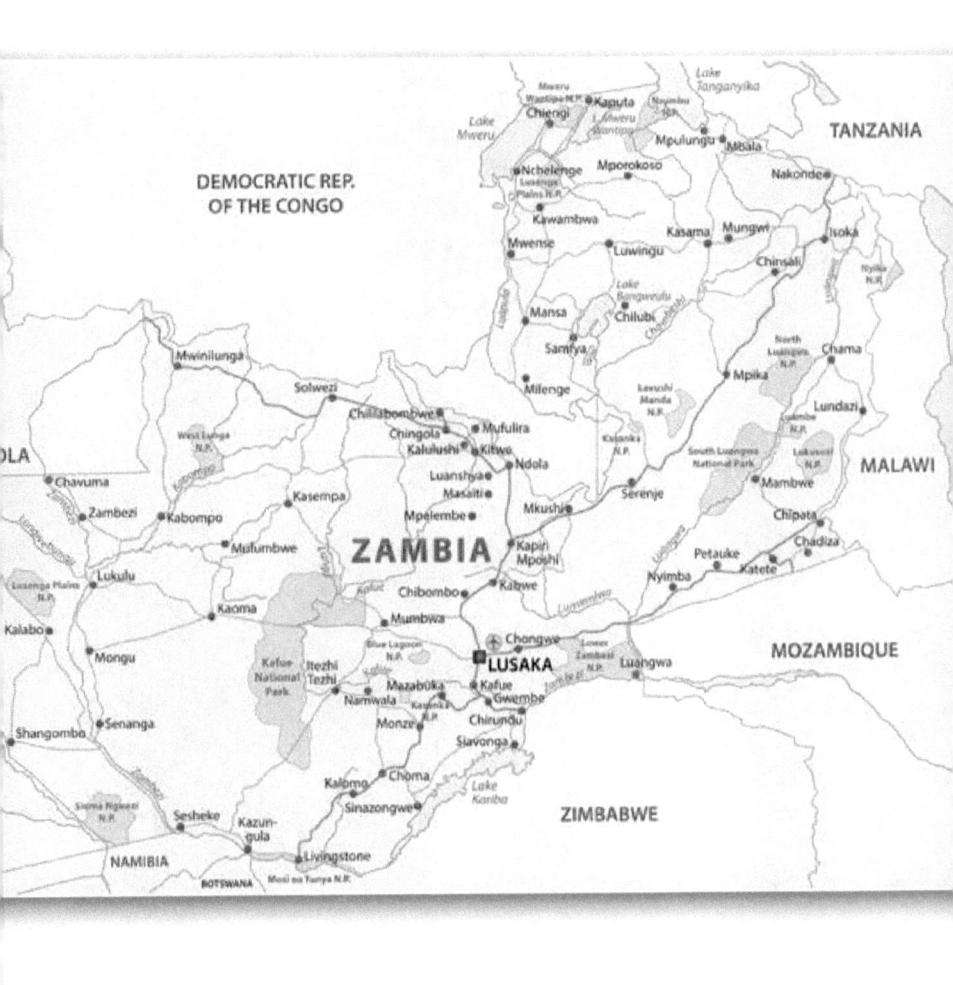

# 1

*Victoria Falls, Southern Africa. 1959*

"Life's not a *joke!*"

Louis Ferreira, a young father, strained away from the railing. He tucked his baby closer to his chest and grasped his five-year-old son's hand. Louis refused to smile but fixed his eyes on the camera operated by his spouse. He repeated his remark and relaxed his hand only when he noticed the boy squirm. Father and son tried their best to appease the photographer. She was adamant to capture more of the Falls in the background and at the same time get her husband and sons to cooperate. It was uncertain whether she would ever abandon her efforts with the Polaroid.

Louis shifted his weight. Why couldn't Maria understand? He could slip on the wet stone-paving while holding the boys. Less than a foot separated them from the abyss behind them with its sheer drop of three hundred feet. They were no longer a carefree couple. Their world had changed. They had responsibilities now. This whole vacation was her idea, despite the fact that there was work to be done—important work.

"Can you two give me *one* proper smile?"

"Maria."

"Mommy!"

"That's it! *One* more." The camera clicked and whirred as the mist and spray from the Falls twirled around them. A gust of wind swept in and made it rain on the family of four. The boy shrieked and struggled to escape the onslaught, but his father's firm grip kept him on the spot. Maria returned the camera to its pouch, swung the strap over her shoulder, and stepped closer to her family with welcoming arms and a beaming face. She was happy with the images she'd taken despite her men's reluctance. She'd put the diaper bag on a chair behind them, far enough from the waterfall spray.

Louis offloaded the still-sleeping baby into his wife's open arms, who made clicking sounds as she transferred the child to her left arm. Her eyes sparkled at her spouse's reluctant grin as she ruffled the older boy's hair the moment he managed to pull free from his father's grip.

"Lukas, why wouldn't you *smile?*" Maria bent down and kissed her oldest son.

Lukas blushed and tried to hide his face in the folds of her skirt. His eyes remained on his parents. He stammered, "Daddy says . . . life is *serious.*"

Maria shot a glance at her husband, who pulled up his shoulders, his face drawn again. *At least somebody was paying attention.*

*There's nothing to explain. The boy's right.* He failed to understand why Maria chose to ignore what was happening around them. The British Federation wasn't even six years old and look what was going on: widespread discontent.

The African people of Northern Rhodesia were unwilling to be ruled much longer by her Majesty. The voices to free themselves from the yoke of the British Empire were getting louder by the day. *Maria should know better.*

*And now this silly vacation.* He loved Maria and his boys, Lukas and Wouter, but when it came to priorities there was no question. The work—the church—always came first. It had to. Then came his family. He had made that clear to Maria the day he'd asked her to follow him into Africa's interior. They were missionaries, first and foremost. It was more than a job, more than an occupation—it was a calling. The solemnity of work was all-encompassing. Faith was crucial, but one's work, one's deeds, weighed more heavily. He found it impossible to shake the belief that his calling was a divine instruction.

"Daddy? Mommy says, *come!*"

At a loss for a moment, Louis spun around, gave his son a halfhearted grin, and took his hand. Maria had taken their younger son, the camera, and the diaper bag and had escaped into the drier interior of the Falls' cafeteria. Louis realized how hungry he was as the aroma from the kitchen wafted over them while he held the door for Lukas.

At an early age, Louis had learned from his father that life was a serious affair. Louis had no scruples about gravitas: it gave structure and surety to one's life. He was instructed in the intricacies of respect before he'd mastered the arts of reading, writing, and multiplying. Life had to be respected as one respected one's parents, any older person, the Reverend, any police officer, the principal, the doctor, the dentist, the judge, and even the tax collector.

He had little time for frivolousness. Maria had not given up, though, trying to get him to relax, to be more laid back. Get him to laugh even. Still, lightheartedness remained foreign to him. He was not convinced of its purpose or its merit. How could he do anything differently if solemnity had been so ingrained into his soul?

The seriousness of being human was a vast subject in of itself, a mystery. He was still coming to grips with his purpose at the age of twenty-nine. Many days he felt trapped in his mortal body. His years at seminary failed to squelch all of his questions. How many times had he tried to explain it to Maria?

She only rolled her eyes at him and claimed he was a disbelieving Thomas. That didn't help. It only opened up another avenue for his troubled heart to wander down. To Maria, life was not a pressing enigma begging to be studied and revered; life was a raging adventure in need of exploration.

How he was going to survive an entire week with his family cooped up in a fancy motel close to the Falls was another mystery. Lukas, for one, would like it, but it would take more than a day (if not a month) for Louis and Maria to get used to being in each other's constant company, in such proximity, for seven days in a row. The process of growing closer to another person had to be phased into with caution, like dipping one's toes into a chilled stream before barging in at the risk of a cramp of the heart muscles.

"*Daddy!*"

He caught up with his family once they reached the tables, amazed at the ease with which Maria always bounced back, irrespective of what life handed to her on a scorching plate. She always seemed unruffled on the surface. He wished he could do that. She beamed and smiled, excusing her party as she weaved with their two children between the people at the tables. They found an open table and plopped down.

Louis thought, *Perhaps I'm responsible for some of her turmoil, what with all my persistence on conviction and principles and doctrines in order to live a pure and honorable life.*

"Louis? The *waiter* wanted to—"

"Oh . . . Sorry."

They placed their order for cold drinks. It was too early for lunch. He regretted skipping breakfast. He just couldn't drag himself out of bed that morning, not on his first free morning of an enforced weeklong vacation. He had instructed Maria to take the children with her and let him be.

The arrangement was to meet up with another missionary couple, the Vermeulens, in an hour's time for an early lunch, at twelve. The moment the waiter stepped away, little Wouter Ferreira woke up. Maria passed the baby to Louis with a wide grin. While still trying to get to the bottom of exactly how their two families happened to be staying at this hotel-slash-motel establishment at the same time, Louis rocked the infant while making shushing sounds to pacify the child. *The coincidence is too big. There has to be collusion. It must be a scheme between Maria and Anna Vermeulen. Phillip would never descend to such a level.* He frowned.

*But should I keep an eye on Maria and Phillip?*

"Here's the bag." Maria handed him their homemade diaper bag. It had always amazed Louis how ingenious Maria could be with a needle and thread and her little Singer machine. There was nothing she wouldn't attempt, and her undertakings always led to remarkable results. The bag looked shop-bought, complete with a waterproof lining. Even the most squeamish dad could feel confident to be seen in public holding such a bag.

As he balanced the now-squealing one-year-old with one arm and held the bright-flowered bag in the other, he whispered. "What about *Lukas*? Who will keep an eye—"

"Oh, *I* will, honey." Maria pulled the wide-eyed Lukas against her side.

Louis hated it when she took advantage of him like that, and especially in public. *That's why we never go out. And she knows it. No wonder she always avoids my father. He's a man of firm principles, of which the fundamental ones are respect and discipline. Later tonight, we'll discuss her public defiance of my position as head of our family. I'm entitled to some respect. And what would happen to Lukas if he wasn't schooled at a young age in all things respect, honor, and discipline? And she shouldn't call me honey in front of strangers. I have a proper name.*

When he returned five minutes later with a more docile infant, soother bobbing between his lips, Louis noticed their table had company. The Vermeulens had joined Maria and Lukas.

They had pulled a second table up close to facilitate visiting. The menfolk always received a firm handshake and the womenfolk a kiss on the lips. That was their custom.

Amidst much laughter, bantering, and patting on the back, Louis shook Philip Vermeulen's hand, as well as the much smaller hand of his four-year-old son, PJ. He detected no uncomfortable glances between Maria, Phillip, or Anna. Perhaps he was an idiot and paranoid without reasonable cause. He felt ashamed. Maria didn't deserve that.

Anna, a woman Maria's age, received a peck on the lips, but Rianna, their eight-year-old, stepped forward with an outstretched hand and shook his hand. She was taller than girls her age. It was clear she would not be kissed. Her dark eyes bore into his.

"Hello, Uncle Louis."

*What is it with this child's intensity?*

He was convinced she would find a kindred spirit in Maria, who had often voiced her objection to this 'kissing of people who were not your family—and then on the *lips!*' He cocked his brow at the girl whose folded arms broadcasted to the world, 'I prefer to sit with the *grootmense*, the adults. I'm almost nine!

## 2

## *Friends. 1959*

Phillip Vermeulen leaned back and sipped on his milkshake. He watched the others through hooded eyes. A grin framed his face. How things had changed. Back in the Fatherland, he would have been sipping a cold beer, although it was too early in the day for that.

On the Mission stations and in the Mission field, it was the unwritten rule: no liquor, no smoking, no fraternizing with staff or the locals, and no cavorting with your neighbor's spouse. He was fine with that. Anna was a vibrant and passionate woman. Her stamina surprised him each time they made love, and he counted his blessings on a regular basis.

He needed this break, this reprieve, and yes, this sweet drink. He had made it as clear as cut crystal to Anna that they could not afford the stay at this swank accommodation, but he had nevertheless agreed upon coming. They both needed to get away—away from the politics and micro-management they were entangled in, exposed to, and forced to endure. They stayed only because they believed this was their calling. He would have it no other way, but it was humbling. They were paid stipends.

He was a trained accountant, but there was only work for so many of them, which had made him decide to become the Station maintenance man. He had taught himself, and he knew he did a good job. The physical labor helped him stay fit and in shape. Anna appreciated his trim physique.

He often berated himself for accepting as inevitable the subtle but no less powerful play of politics in their own Missions body. He often thought, *Why wasn't I deemed good enough or qualified enough to perform the duties I was trained for. And why are we sent across the field to a new posting, often on a week's notice, all on the whims of a committee?* He had six months outstanding on the completion of his practicum when he had received the call to the Missions. He became convinced he had to leave the firm he'd been working for in the Cape. If he had opted to stay, he would have been partner by now, a chartered accountant with his own office featuring a floor-to-ceiling window looking out over the Indian Ocean.

He eyed Rianna, the shining apple of his eye. She was unaware of his scrutiny. She sat somewhat apart. It was clear to everyone in the party, Lukas and PJ included, that she would have nothing to do with the *kleintjies*, the little ones. She had requested a Hubbly-Bubbly float and pushed the island of ice cream around with her straw, eating nibbles of it with the tip of the straw. Her mop of red curls covered her eyes and upper body, making it easier to keep to herself. Usually she sat upright like a meerkat on lookout, always curious—this was her sulking position.

*Perhaps I should reprimand the child? She shouldn't grow up wild.*

He had heard word among the local *Chinyanja* people that she was fast becoming a prolific tree climber. Her forte was scaling mango trees, apparently. They whispered she was a legend in the making. He only scoffed when they told him. It was uncommon in their culture for girls to climb trees, and so much more for a white *Amissioni* girl to take a liking to it. Whether it was the sweet yellow fruit that lured her or the sheer glory of disappearing into a dark-green world of her own, high above everyone else on the Station, he couldn't fathom.

*If only she would grow up to be a lady like her mother, then I'd sleep more soundly at night.*

He glanced across the table at Louis Ferreira, the reverend minister. How much did he have to do with this arrangement of them being here together for the entire week at the Falls? Something didn't add up. The Stations were far apart, their salaries small, and resources for gasoline were restricted. The result was that they saw one another on average only four times a year for meetings and then again at Christmas, and, on occasion, someone's birthday.

Ferreira was a pleasant enough fellow—once he managed to relax and turn off his obsession with the sanctity of work and man's predestined place in God's mysterious creation. He also knew the man was a sworn supporter of Millennialism, or Chiliasm, the teaching of a thousand-year reign of Christ following the Second

Coming. Apparently this prediction was five years overdue according to their calculations, and Ferreira was quick to remind them of this belief. He knew Ferreira had been instructed by the Mission's Secretary, Dr. Rossouw, to keep those sentiments to himself. The Chinyanja people had no need for that.

He suspected Ferreira of belonging to the secret inner circle of the 'committee.' This enabled him to land postings at more exotic locations.

Phillip knew it could lead to a confrontation if he got the man too fired up or questioned his commitment. It might even end in a fistfight or a rift in the local Mission body. Rather, it would be best and safest to inquire about his thoughts on the latest building projects that the Mission's Secretary had approved. Louis Ferreira loved building churches.

*But it can wait.*

Phillip smiled and nodded at no one in particular. He was content. The children were behaving, little Wouter was asleep again, the women were chatting, and Louis was keeping to himself. He would nurse his shake to make it last.

*We can talk later. This week next to the Falls should not be wasted on work-related concerns.*

"Excuse me, *Bwana* Phil."

Phillip Vermeulen snapped out of his daydreaming. *Why did Louis always address me as Mister Phil? Why the damn formality?* He forced a smile as he leaned closer. *The man should really pull that broomstick from his behind.* "Hello, Louis."

"*Bwana* Phil, did you have a look at this month's Mission News?"

Phillip Vermeulen nodded.

"What do you think about the new church building planned for Magwero?"

Phillip straightened out. Ferreira had his full attention. He had thought it a misprint when he'd read it and paid it no heed. There was already a church building at that particular Station in Magwero. "Why was a *second* church building approved?"

Ferreira brimmed with excitement. He pushed his empty glass out of the way. "To replace the *old* one with something better! The new one is twice the size, allows three times the amount of natural light than the old, and it's to celebrate the church planting—"

"It's a mistake. I was in Magwero a month ago and attended a service in that church. The place was in a pristine condition—"

"That's not the point, *Bwana* Phil. The new one will be improved. It will be safer."

"*Who* approved it?" Phillip asked, his brows furrowed and his jaw twitched. "There's *no* money."

Louis laughed, shrugging his shoulders. "The Mission's Secretary, of course."

"Well, he's made an error of judgment. They don't *need* a second church." He felt Anna's eyes on him. He had to lower his voice. He glanced in her direction and gave her a quick smile when she made her eyes big at him. He knew she didn't trust his made-up smiles. What she didn't appreciate is that he hadn't even mentioned to Ferreira how shockingly far behind the corporate body of the Dutch Reformed Church in Zambia was with paying their missionaries a living wage. It was a disgrace—all these secret dealings behind closed doors. *And it was always justified with the pacifying phrase, 'Because it's for the work of the Lord.'*

"Brother Phil, the new building will enable the congregation to serve the Lord better—"

"Oh, bollocks! Dr. Rossouw should concern himself with paying us a living wage rather than erecting a second, grander building."

Phillip jumped up, then sat down when he heard Anna murmur his name. He avoided her gaze. *I should leave before I lose my temper.* Part of him wanted to lean across the table and slap the educated reverend to get some sense into him. *The sheer impudence of the man. The glaring ignorance.* Maintenance personnel received a 20 percent lower income than the missionaries. And the missionaries already received little.

Ferreira placed his hands together in front of him in a prayer-like position. "Phillip, the money to build this new church is for the work of the Lord—"

*Enough*! Phillip snapped out of his seat, hands gripping the edges of the table. He leaned toward the reverend, their faces inches apart. He hissed. "Don't give me that holier-than-though bullshit! It comes out of the pockets of those poor congregation members. Most of them live under the breadline. How can you justify another cathedral?"

Ferreira scoffed. "*Cathedrals*? They're simple red-brick structures with metal roofs."

"Oh, they're fancy enough! *Excuse* me!" Philip spun around, gave Anna a sideways glance, and stomped from the cafeteria.

Rianna had also jumped up and stepped closer to her mother. She was ready to follow her father. Both Maria and Anna glanced at Louis with raised brows. Maria had been paying attention to Wouter in her lap and listening to Anna, so she'd missed most of the interaction between the two men.

"Mommy, I'll go and make sure he's okay," Rianna said, ready to bolt.

Anna stood. "Thank you, darling, that's not your job. Stay with PJ. I'll go and find your dad." She hugged her daughter, gave Maria a brave smile, and followed in the direction that her husband had taken off.

Maria pushed her chair back and clutched the baby to her chest. "I'm *ashamed* of you!"

Louis leaned back in his chair as he glanced at his spouse. He stammered, "*What?*" He had never anticipated such a reaction. *What did I do wrong? I only informed Phillip Vermeulen about the new church building planned for Magwero.*

"She's my *friend*! *They* are my friends. Where's your compassion?"

He said nothing, shook his head, and begged her with his eyes to lower her voice lest she make an even bigger scene. After moving the now-awake boy to her other hip, she continued. "Go *find* him. *Apologize*."

"But Maria, he—"

"No buts! If you *don't*, then I'm taking the children this minute. We'll get a taxi, take the train, and return to the Missions station. I'll pack and travel the two thousand miles back to South Africa. We'll stay there until you come to your senses."

Louis jumped up with a nervous laugh. "You won't really do that."

Maria stepped back and took Lukas by the hand.

Rianna sat next to her brother, three chairs away, huddled together. Her brooding eyes bored through him.

Maria thrust out her chin, her face drawn. "This ends *now*. I'm so tired of all the hypocrisy. You preach the gospel, but there's so little compassion—only cold dogma."

Her eyes were moist. She let go of Lukas's hand and pointed toward the exit.

# 3

## The need for peace. 1959

Louis spent the next hour tracking down Phillip Vermeulen. Exhausted and ready to give up, Louis found him on a lookout balcony a hundred steps down. The going was slow as perpetual spray had drenched the stairs. One had to be cautious. The roar of the water made talking difficult. Several times, he tried to get the man to understand.

Louis shuddered and staggered back, repulsed by his thoughts: *it would be so easy to push the man.* He gasped, mortified, and hurried back, clinging like a blind man to the wet railing.

Despite his apology, the atmosphere between the two men remained strained. That a chill would appear between him and Maria stunned him. It hurt. Yet, he couldn't be convinced that he had committed a deadly sin. She was, once again, making an Everest out of a modest molehill. He failed to grasp why she remained so upset, even vowing to separate from him. The church would never give its blessing. A divorce would be devastating to the progress they'd made to win the hearts of the local Chinyanjas. *We have to set an example.*

Anna and Maria did their best to heal the rift. They visited with each other several times a day as Lukas and PJ played together, unconcerned about the conundrum between the adults.

Rianna, wise for her years, shadowed her father and, on display for all, declared her unconditional loyalty. She made it clear she would protect him. Her dark eyes would stare at Louis, challenging him without a word.

By the fifth day Maria had insisted they return home. The Falls had lost its charm—its grandiosity and ever-present mist were unable to clear and heal the minds and hearts of its visitors this time.

———

Life on the Station was busy and demanded Louis's attention. There was little time for him to worry about the ill feelings of others. There was work to do—important work—the work of the Lord. He had to get the plans for the new church building in Magwero ready. He didn't need Phillip Vermeuelen's blessing.

Louis had trained as a city planner before attending Seminary and had briefed the Mission's Secretary on the matter when Louis had accepted the call to the Mission Field. He knew how to draw plans. He'd also completed an entire year of structural engineering before he'd switched to drawing plans.

It helped that the Stations were far apart. Now he didn't have to look into more accusing eyes—his wife's were enough.

Phillip had never allowed Louis to explain the true reason for the new church building: safety. Structural flaws in the existing building had been discovered weeks earlier. Part of the roof and an entire sidewall was in danger of caving in. Repair wasn't a viable option.

He had tried to explain that to Maria, but she wouldn't listen. Since the fiasco at the Falls, she hadn't allowed him even to touch her, but she'd stopped short of sleeping in a different room. She allowed him a peck on her cheek, probably for the children's sake. Well, for Lukas's sake.

Only this morning he had breached the subject again, hoping for a breakthrough, to prove he was not as callous as she accused him of and that he had no ill motive.

"Maria," he said, "Would you take another look at this photograph?" He held out a recent image of the church.

She refused to take it.

"*You* and the Old Man have been colluding on this for months!" She snorted loudly as she changed her mind, pulled the image from his fingers, and studied the photo. "I see *nothing* the matter with it. And you made it sound as if we had a second Tower of Pisa on our hands!" She returned the picture. "I see no cracks in the walls. They're nice and straight, and the roof is as firm as always!"

He sighed. "You have to look *closer*, from *inside* the building, *inside* the roof. You have to crawl up there. If you *know* what to look for, it's—"

"So now I'm *stupid?*

"No. You're a smart woman."

She shrugged her shoulders. She studied him long and hard. "If, and it's a big if—if there are structural defects—why didn't you *tell* Phil?"

"I tried!"

"You did *not* try hard enough! Why all this nonsense about celebrating the church planting and about the congregation who will serve the Lord better?"

"But it's all true!"

"Bollocks, *Louis Ferreira!* You have to make right with him."

"I spoke to the man that same afternoon! And again, before we left the Falls."

Maria shook her head then gazed down at her hands. When she faced him, her eyes were moist. "You may think this is a silly and unimportant issue. You're mistaken. This has repercussions for all of us. It's about trust and respect and compassion. You've violated these principles."

Louis lurched forward. "That's not true!" He considered going to her chair. She wasn't one to shed tears without reason.

"Are you aware that Phil was a semester short of becoming a chartered accountant when they received the calling?"

"And I'm a qualified city planner!"

She shook her head and wiped over her eyes. "You have changed . . . Missions don't pay us much, but they pay the maintenance staff even less. Phil was right: there's money for churches. I don't know how your boss, the *Oubaas*, sleeps at night."

Louis jumped from his stool and paced the room, his hands clasped behind his back. "First, my boss isn't that old. Second, that's why we have a Treasurer, why we have regular meetings, we follow the bylaws, adhere to the church order—"

"Like the Pharisees."

"Maria!"

"I've never thought of you as a cold-hearted bastard."

"Why do you mock me?"

"I'm afraid of what I see, of what I hear."

He turned, stepped closer, and touched her shoulder. She jerked away as if his hand had scorched her. She jumped to her feet and stepped away. "This won't go away. It's a cancer. It has to be surgically removed—"

"*What* are you talking about?"

"Wake up, Reverend Ferreira! You will *not* share my bed. You will drive over to Katete and go make peace with the Vermeulens . . . Learn some compassion."

"I told you, I have—"

"Then talk to Phil at this weekend's Missions meeting."

"I'll think about—"

"You're so *blind!*" Maria gave a sob and stumbled from the room, her hand clasped to her mouth.

Louis Ferreira remained in the room.

*Too bad about Maria. I'll have to speak to her this evening, make her understand that she'll have to change her attitude. She, like so many of the others in the Field, understands so little about living a spirit-filled life. They're content with living a mediocre life.*

*My father was right—it all starts with respect. Respect for the head of the household. Respect for the ordained of the Lord. Respect for the church. Respect for the authority of the church. I'm ordained. I'm the head of this house. I understand the prophecies. She has so little understanding of the Scriptures and what it means to honor your husband. Perhaps I should pity her. Like I pity Phillip.*

Louis sighed and went to his study. He had a sermon to prepare.

*Life's not a joke.*

———

Maria was not one to make idle threats, and she spoke her mind without squirming. She moved to their spare bedroom that same afternoon.

Minutes before their evening meal, Louis went to that spare bedroom. *We have to talk.* He stood outside the door, hesitant to knock. *This has never happened to us before.* He knocked with caution.

"It's open."

He poked his head in the door. There was lead in her voice.

She had moved Wouter's cot and a small mattress for Lukas to sleep on next to her bed. She gave him a feeble smile and continued folding clothes which she then packed into an open suitcase lying on the bed.

"Maria. *What* are you doing?"

She shrugged her shoulders and slipped the soother into Wouter's mouth when he started wailing.

Lukas gave no indication he was aware of the tension between his parents and ran to his father. For a moment Louis clung to his son. *What's happening to us?*

The dining room bell sounded down the hallway. The *Cooky* was ready, and it was his privilege to ring the minuscule brass bell.

The practice in the Field was for the local *Chinyanja* people to come work for the *Amissioni* as house servants. In spite of the hope throughout the country, that their future would improve once they could rid themselves from their British yoke, the *Chinyanja's* traditional way of living was fast eroding. Work was scarce. Even working as house servants for the white *Amissioni* was better than going hungry. The missionaries had little money, but they could still afford to pay servants.

A work ranking order existed in these grand old houses that the missionaries lived in—remnants of the glory days of the British colonial era. The most coveted position was that of the *Cooky*, who was responsible for the kitchen and every meal. The second-in-command was the house boy, responsible for every-thing indoors, excluding the domain of the *Cooky*. Least coveted was that of the *bwalo boy*, the gardener, who was responsible for everything else and everything outside. It was only the men who came to work for the missionaries in their households.

Louis had stepped inside the bedroom and scooped Lukas up. "*Where* will you be going?"

The supper bell sounded a second time.

Maria held the squirming baby in her arms. "To Lusaka—*with* the children. Come. That was the *second* bell." She touched Lukas's cheek in passing.

She called down the hallway, "We're *coming*, Philemon! *Zikomo!* Thank you!" She called over her shoulders. "Lukas, run along and wash your hands."

Louis took her elbow as they entered the dining room. He whispered when he noticed the *Cooky* on the other side of the room, waiting for them to sit down. "*Why* didn't you tell me?"

"I'm telling you *now*."

"But *why* are you going?"

"We'll talk later." She smiled at Philemon and sat down with Wouter still in her arms. Philemon stepped forward and maneuvered the infant's high chair closer. He took the boy from her, slipped him onto the chair, and strapped him in place on the stool. Lukas joined them, wiping his hands dry on his pants as Philemon placed the dishes in the middle of the table.

———

It was two hours later by the time the two boys were fed, bathed, and put to bed—in the spare bedroom.

Louis knocked again on the half-open door.

"Come in, Louis."

She went to him when he entered. Surprised by all of this he opened his arms and pulled her close. He nestled his face in her hair. She was on bare feet and he was still half-an-inch shorter. He shuddered and held her tight. Her breasts pressed into him.

*How long had it been? And dear Lord, what am I doing to us?*

"Maria . . . I love you."

"Then you'll let us go."

"But why go?"

"For you to come to your senses. This is not an idle threat—"

"Where are you going to stay?"

"In the Mission Rest house."

Louis laughed, uncertain about the implications. He held her at arm's length. "Dr. Rossouw will hear about your visit. He would want to know what's going on and—"

"What should I tell him if I run into him?" She challenged him and held his eyes. He'd never seen this side of her. He shook his shoulders as if to shed a load off his back.

"Maria, be *reasonable*."

"It's been *three* months. You've refused to take the situation to heart. You live in your parallel universe, in this holier-than-thou utopia." She sobbed and turned away.

He stepped closer and pulled her closer again.

She spun around and thumped with clenched fists against his chest. "Come down from the mountain, Moses . . . Please. I love you, but it can't continue like this!"

"What do you expect me to do?"

"You have *two* weeks. If I don't hear from Anna Vermeulen, and preferably from Phil himself, that peace has been brokered— I'm talking about an honest reconciliation, in person—the three of us will be off to the South."

"*Maria*. I try so hard . . . I subject myself to the highest standards. I live a disciplined and righteous life. I strive to be good—"

"Step down from the mountain."

"What do you mean? I'm standing here, right *next* to you."

"Don't try to be good—you're not a god. Learn *compassion*. *Be* compassionate."

"Maria."

"Good night, Louis."

# 4

*Making peace. 1959*

Maria insisted in her quiet way that Louis drop her and the children off at the train station. The journey to Lusaka would last the best part of six hours. She had refused to back down from her plan to sleep in the guest bedroom. Louis had to sleep alone for the first time in seven years. If he had refused to drive them, she would have hailed a taxi—so he drove them.

Philemon, the *cooky*, and Cecil, the house boy, went about their tasks that morning as if the *Amayi* and the little ones went on a train ride every Wednesday. When Louis helped Maria into the vehicle and handed her the baby, their eyes met, again. His were red, hollow, with blue rings—he hadn't slept the night. Maria's were moist. She tried her best to smile. She shook her head, her eyes wide. They seemed to say, *Close the door, Louis. I've made up my mind.*

Between them the unspoken lay bared, uncomfortable and perilous—a bundle of dynamite sticks wrapped together. In the backseat, Lukas chattered about everything he saw through the side window. After all, he was going on a train ride with Mommy and Wouter.

Maria and Louis didn't exchange a single word on the way to the station. Not until she was on the train did either of them speak.

Maria made Lukas hold his brother as she fought the wide window open, pushing it all the way down, while Louis scuttled outside when the conductor's first whistle sounded. He stood on tiptoes outside their window and reached for her hand. Maria leaned halfway out the window, careful to keep the child against her chest, her free hand entwined with Louis's.

"Maria, don't leave—"

"It's better this way."

"I'll *halt* the plans for the new church on Magwero!"

"It's not about Magwero."

"I'll phone Dr. Rossouw. Magwero can wait."

"No, it can't. The report is out: you don't want a church building collapsing on the congregation."

"It's not safe on the trains anymore. The country is changing."

"Stop worrying about *us*, Louis! You know what *you* have to go and fix."

The conductor's second whistle startled her. Wouter started crying. The train chucked. Louis had both hands now inside the window and kept pace with the moving train. He walked faster. He tried to touch Lukas's hand as well. "Goodbye, Lukas!"

"Goodbye, Daddy!"

The train chucked again, harder. Maria and the child fell back against the seat. She scrambled forward, fighting for balance.

Louis's hand was still holding on to the frame, as he was now running beside the train.

"I love you, Maria!"

"My love." She touched his fingers as he lost his grip on the window when the train lurched forward. Maria and Lukas leaned out the window and waved at his receding figure. He was the only one who stood at the very end of the platform, a stooped figure.

Mother and son stared and waved until they both got soot in their eyes, making them tear and laugh. Maria made Lukas hold the baby again as she wrestled the window closed. *It would be better to keep it closed.* Wouter was inconsolable and only settled down when she sat and gave him the breast.

Lukas sat across from them, fascinated at his brother making suckling noises as he clasped his mother's breast with his round little fists. Maria had no scruples to let her son see her feed his brother. She had always thought it to be beautiful and natural. No fuss was required. She knew Louis would have had a fit. He would have insisted she use a throw over her upper body and the child, to cover her shame. *What should I be mortified of?* Even after two babies her breasts had not lost their luster. *And why did the good Lord think it wise to give me two if it's a sin to be proud of them?*

*It's time for those men who trot around with solemn faces and dressed in their black suits, white shirts, and white ties to think about the implications of all their Synod decisions. Less rules and bylaws are needed. The people need less organized religion. They're in desperate need for compassion. It's time for all of them to examine their hearts and motives.*

She leaned against the backrest and closed her eyes. She listened as the steam engine chucked harder. The click-clack of the rails always consoled her. Lukas scuttled across the narrow space between the seats and nestled in on her side, tickling his brother's feet.

Maria pulled him tightly against her side as she cuddled his brother in the hook of her arm while readjusting her nipple in his mouth. Together they listened to the click-clack.

She sighed. *Poor Louis. Poor Dr. Rossouw.* She pictured his drawn face when he would receive the news: *Bwana Ferreira's spouse, with their two children—Yes! Can you believe it?—had jumped on a steam locomotive to Lusaka!*

She was traveling with a year-old baby and a five-year-old boy because she was in disagreement about how her husband executed his duties in the Field. She might be placed under church discipline.

Maria was startled from her daydreaming by a rattle outside their compartment door.

"Tickets!" Another rattle followed on the door clip.

"Coming!" Maria scampered upright, pushed the baby in Lukas's arms, and retrieved their tickets from her purse. She unlocked the clip and pulled the door open.

The train jerked and made them all stumble, fighting for balance. The conductor lurched forward and bumped into her. "Pardon me, Ma'am!" He straightened himself out and pushed his uniform cap back on his head as he seized her up and down. "Tickets. Ma'am?"

Maria felt his eyes on her chest and buttoned her dress higher up. *What is he thinking?* She was annoyed with herself and felt the crimson rising in her neck. She jabbed the tickets in front of her to get his eyes off her breasts. *Isn't he too young to be a conductor? Shouldn't he still be in school?* She could tell he was fit and trim by the way he carried himself; he was too certain of himself. He smelled of soap and sun—clean and vibrant.

"Thank you, Ma'am." His eyes lowered to her chest again. She followed his gaze, her face crimson by now. Her nipples were jutting against her cool summer dress. She clasped her arms across her chest and stepped toward the door, forcing him back and out of the compartment.

"Where is the *bwana?*" The smirk never left his face. His dark eyes sparkled. He had a dimple in his chin.

"There's no *bwana*. Now please *leave* us." She pulled her clipped tickets from his hand and reached for the door.

"Yes, Ma'am."

She slammed the door shut, locked it, and leaned against it, closing her eyes. Her breathing came fast. *The boys!* Lukas sat at the window with Wouter on his lap, who had a soother in his little mouth. Both smiled at her. *Thank God!*

———

Philemon the *cooky* had packed them a lunch basket. Following their meal at the D-shaped table that rested on top of the petite hand basin between the two windows, Maria breast-fed Wouter a second time. She couldn't say why, but this time she draped a clean diaper halfway across her chest. She remained aware of Lukas's eyes on her and the baby the entire time.

*Click!*

Maria must have fallen asleep. She jerked upright when the lock unclipped, the door slid open, and the young conductor stepped inside with a wide grin. Lukas lay on his side, asleep. Even Wouter had dozed off in his small carrycot underneath the fold-down table.

"*What* do you want?" Maria balled her fists as she perched on the front of the bench.

He grinned at her with the whitest teeth she'd ever seen. "I have time off. I thought I might come and keep the *Amayi* company. She is alone. I see the *mwanas* are asleep. That is good. Yes?" Again, the flashing smile.

Maria jumped from her seat. She didn't want to wake the boys. She lowered her voice. "Get *out!*" She held her fists in front of her and inched closer.

The young man laughed and took hold of her wrists. "I won't hurt you, Ma'am." As she resisted his advance she felt his hands lock around her wrists. He was strong. Fear choked her throat. *My God. Louis. The boys.*

Maria winced with discomfort as the man pulled her toward him. "*One* kiss."

"*No!*" Maria hollered as she snapped her arms free, shoving the man backward.

Her force had surprised her assailant. The confined space didn't help. He fell sideways onto the opposite bench but hurled himself erect and came in with more force, for a hug this time, arms wider. Maria brought her knee up with all her might as he got hold of her and tried to press her against him.

"*Help*! Let *go* of me!"

The man groaned as her knee came up again and this time made contact with his groin, but he didn't let go. They fell onto the opposite bench as his mouth, now inches from her face, sought her lips.

Wouter hollered murder and Lukas chimed in with a shrill, "*Mommy!* What's the man doing? Let *go* of my Mommy!"

Everyone on the train must have heard the boys, all the way down to the locomotive.

A new voice, a man's, reverberated throughout the compartment. "*Zikuyenda?*" Maria stumbled to her feet as the stranger pulled the young man off of her.

"Let *go* of her!"

A thwack followed as her rescuer's fist struck her attacker's chin, sending him sprawling through the door, into the corridor, and crashing into the outside wall of the carriage. The baby screamed without taking a breath, and Lukas sat by the window bawling even more loudly.

Maria straightened out her dress, pulled her fingers through her hair, picked up her youngest, and plopped down next to Lukas, soothing both boys. Her eyes never left the two fighting men. Her chest heaved as she fought for control.

Her rescuer had wrestled the other man down to the floor and into the corridor. He'd ripped the attacker's belt out of his pants and tied his hands behind his back. Her rescuer leaned into the compartment and asked, "Did he molest you, Ma'am?"

Maria sniffed, wiping her eyes and fighting to stop shaking. "Yes," she whispered, close to inaudible. *How am I going to explain the bruises on my arms to Dr. Rossouw? Or to Louis?*

Lukas chimed in, "That man *hurt* Mommy!"

Their rescuer gave the molester another smack against the side of his head, stood up from the floor, and stepped closer. He filled the entire doorway as he grinned at her and the boys. He was tall and broad-shouldered. He looked Lukas in the eye and said, "Don't worry. He won't do that to your mommy anymore."

He made a half salute in her direction, threw a quick glance at his captive, then stepped forward and put out his hand. "I am Charles Chombe, at your service, Ma'am."

Maria scrambled to her feet and took the offered hand. "*Thank you*, Mr. Chombe. I'm Maria Ferreira, and these are my sons, Lukas and Wouter. You have been ... so kind to us."

Lukas slipped off the bench and shook the tall *Chinynaja's* hand with both hands, a wide grin on his tear-streaked face. "*Zikomo kwambiri*, Charles!" he piped. "Thank you very much!"

———

Maria and the children arrived in Lusaka in one piece. Charles Chombe had taken it upon himself for the rest of the trip to stand guard outside at a discreet distance away down the hallway from their compartment. After arriving in Lusaka, and after handing over the disgraced conductor to the station authorities, Charles ensured their safe arrival at the Rest House, despite her objections.

Three years would pass before she set eyes on Charles Chombe again.

She received a call from Anna Vermeulen from Katete, three days after her arrival in Lusaka. Within minutes both women were in tears.

"What's *wrong*? Why are you crying?" Maria asked.

"I'm so relieved ..." Anna said, sniffing.

"Then what is Louis still *doing* there? Did he have engine trouble? Did he have a *meltdown*?" Maria asked.

"No!" Anna laughed through her sobs. "They're both fine. There's nothing the matter with his vehicle. It's dark out—so we've decided he's staying over. It had taken them that long—yes, the entire day, to make peace."

"What time did Louis get there?"

Another chuckle from Anna. "We were still at the breakfast table—he said he couldn't sleep."

"They've been talking the *entire* day?" Maria asked.

"For the most part."

"What else did they do?" Maria said.

"It was Louis who broke down first. He cried. Later, Phil started crying too."

"Phil cried?"

"He did. But I thought he was coming to get his lever-action Marlin and shoot the *bwana*. They were that angry. They shouted at one another," Anna said.

"What about?"

"Everything—the church, the DRC . . . and the *Afrikaner Broederbond* and why they left South Africa. They talked about why they were in Missions."

Anna went quiet. She sniffled before she continued. "Maria . . . What does the AB have to do with them, with us, being in Northern Rhodesia?"

"I'm not sure."

"Well . . . Then they shouted some more. It was only later, in the afternoon that they calmed down. That's when the weeping started."

Anna started sobbing again. "I didn't know Louis could *cry*. He's always so strong. He's always been this perfect . . . this holy man."

Maria laughed through her tears. "I told him to come down from the mountain."

"I think he has," Anna murmured.

# 5

*Putting a hunting party together is what good friends do. 1962*

Once peace was made, Louis Ferreira and Phil Vermeulen found valid reasons to visit and see each other once a month instead of every three. Their head office in Lusaka required them to justify and log their transportation expenses. This all followed Maria's impromptu train trip to Lusaka with the two boys. In the end, she had only stayed for a week. Perhaps that is the reason she never ran into Dr. Rossouw. The bruises on her arms had disappeared by the time she'd gone home.

Maria chastised herself for being jealous of the new friendship that had sprouted between the two men. They showed Anna Vermeulen, herself, and the rest of the staff what true camaraderie looked like. They became inseparable, like David and Jonathan.

The *Chinyanjas* only shook their heads at the *Amissioni*, the strange people from the South. And the two *bwanas* were even stranger, they said. The one day they yelled at each other while brandishing their rifles, and the next day they couldn't stop hugging one another. *Nditho!*

For two Christmases in a row following the reconciliation, Maria had to listen to the men talk about the epic hunt they were planning. It was epic because of the prized target and its symbolism of their new forged friendship. Their sights were set high. They didn't consider hunting graceful antelopes like the elusive bushbuck, with its striped back and spotted flanks, or the majestic kudu, with its twisting spiraled horns. Those weren't considered valuable enough for what the men had in mind.

It had to be a buffalo: an African buffalo.

Maria rolled her eyes at their talk and thought nothing of it. Once a year the men went hunting, but for antelope. Bringing an impala, a kudu, or an eland home was no small feat. *This epic hunt is only talk. Nothing will come of it.* She knew, as everyone living in the bush knew: hunting the African buffalo, the Cape buffalo, was not for amateurs.

She was a wise enough woman not to use the word amateur in front of Louis, or even Phil. And yet, the *Chinyanjas* had a reason they called the grown bull the *wakuda kufa*, the Black Death. At two thousand pounds or more, the African savannah buffalo, with its unpredictable nature, had little trouble goring people to death. Each year, two hundred people were killed by these animals, who were on any day as dangerous as the hippopotamus and the crocodile. She paid little heed to the men's daydreaming. Those majestic animals with their wide sweeping horns were for professional hunters—not for hobbyists, and especially not for preachers, church builders, and maintenance men.

Maria was wrong.

The men were serious. It started with target shooting in Katete. Louis must have realized he could enjoy more freedom out from under Maria's watchful eyes. By the beginning of April that year, once a week on Saturday afternoons they would go out to their makeshift range and shoot for an hour. The plan for the hunt was to go in late Fall during the last weekend of May.

Target shooting was only the beginning. Then they went for runs, all the way down to the river and back up the long hill—a kilometer long. Five times. Anna Vermeulen always phoned Maria early Saturday evenings, filling her in on the men's progress. At night, Louis did push-ups and sit-ups in their bedroom before retiring.

The *Chinyanjas* stopped shaking their heads as they now gawked at the two *bwanas*. *Do they suffer from a new form of brain malaria?*

After these runs the men carried boulders the size of watermelons, weighing in at fifty pounds each.

"Perhaps it's brain malaria *and* bilharzia," the locals whispered.

Maria considered writing a letter to Dr. Rossouw in Lusaka. Perhaps he should be made aware of how his fellow missionaries whiled away their time, if only to prevent them from pursuing this half-baked plan to kill a buffalo. He had the authority to stop them, even if under a false pretense.

Or she could ask Dr. Brown, the old physician, to insist that the men all pay him a visit and verify they were of sound mind.

Perhaps this was an early sign of the elusive but much dreaded "nervous breakdown" they'd always heard about. All the workers in the Field knew that working year after year in the hinterland of Africa was not for opportunists or the weak-hearted. Such work demanded nerves of forged steel, utter perseverance, and hard-headedness beyond the sensible range.

It's still uncertain how the target-shooting, hill-running, boulder-carrying men stumbled upon the tracking talents of the young *Chinyanja*, Charles Chombe. Perhaps it was Ulrich Wessels who had discovered him; he was also from Madzi Moyo, where Charles worked as house boy at the school hostel. Charles's dream was to become a teacher one day, but he'd found work at the hostel, hoping to save enough to go back to school—one day.

Charles had learned how to track animals from his father as a young boy. Reading the spoor—the trail, scent, or droppings of a wild animal—required little second guessing for the house boy.

The first time they met in Katete next to the shooting range, Louis took an instant liking to the young man towering over him.

"*Moni, Mbusa,*" the man said.

"*Moni*, Charles! *Muli bwanyi?*" Louis wanted to know how the young man was doing and appreciated Charles's respect for his title of *Mbusa*—pastor.

He recalled Maria's rendition of the friendly giant who had saved her from the hands of the troubled train conductor—it didn't do justice to the man's hand he shook. Louis found it difficult to believe that this self-confident man who carried himself with such ease was content working as a house boy.

The men couldn't wait to share their plans of the buffalo hunt with Charles. They sang his praises and made it clear why they needed a capable tracker.

As the good-natured man he was, he only laughed and said, "I would be honored to accompany you, but first I must discuss your offer with my boss at the school hostel."

At their second meeting a week later, Charles asked if he could introduce them to a childhood friend, a master spoor-reader—a true tracker more worthy of the title. Charles had already spoken to the friend.

Pemba Chiluba was the physical opposite of his friend Charles: he was a soft-spoken, shy man of lesser stature. They'd grown up in the same village and later on the same farm. When Charles found employment with the *Amissioni*, Pemba discovered he could hire out his skills to professional hunters. Muscles weren't required for such a job—only alert eyes and knowing what to look for. Pemba got busy making a name for himself, and he preferred the hunters from America because they were willing to pay. The income would probably never make him a rich man, but it kept food on the table.

———

Soon, word about the monumental buffalo hunt got out, and two other missionaries, Ulrich Wessels and Kobus Kok, were lured to join the budding hunting party. Louis, the unofficial spokesperson, made it clear that practice shooting wasn't optional. Except for the tracker, each one in the party had to carry a rifle and know how to use it.

For the first time in months, the conversation at the communal dinner table Saturday evening didn't circle back to what the ANC and UNIP parties were doing in preparation for dismantling the British Federation. Rather, the talk centered on which rifle was the all-around best for hunting African big game.

Phil Vermeulen drew the line in the red sand about which rifle was *verboten*. To make his point, he jumped up at the head of the dinner table. "Gentlemen, show of hands. Who owns a four-fifty-eight Winchester?"

The men laughed and shook their heads.

"You all make me so proud! The old Winchester is too unreliable. We can't take any chances with a Cape Buffalo."

"I'm definitely taking my four-sixteen Rigby," Ulrich Wessels said.

This time it was Louis Ferreira who waved the men to order. "Then we'll make *you* form the rear-guard with your *big* buffalo rifle."

"It's like a bazooka. It's more of an elephant rifle!" piped Kobus Kok, while the men cheered the now embarrassed Ulrich Wessels.

"Then it's a done deal, gentlemen," said Phil. "Ulrich's *bazooka* will work out quite grand with our three-seventy-five H and H Magnums. All we need now is a good tracker to find us our wide-horned bull and we're set!"

They knew it was critical to carry a gun they were comfortable with but also one able to penetrate the thick skin of one of Africa's most dangerous bovines. With only a single round in the chamber, the power to stop a charging two-thousand-pound beast would make all the difference in the world.

———

At the end of April, Louis got home from his target shooting and "men's retreat," as Maria called it now. She took him to task.

"Why can't you be satisfied with an eland bull?"

"I've shot one before."

"Then get a permit for a kudu."

"Maria, I did that the year before."

"The savannah buffalo is not for the occasional hunter. It's best left for the professionals."

"Haven't you seen how we've been practicing? Are you not paying attention?" he asked with mocked disgust. "We're this close to *professionals*."

She scoffed, elbowing him in the ribs.

"It's not the same," she whispered. "I can't shake it, Louis— I'm afraid this time."

He pulled her closer and kissed her hair. "Don't be. We've obtained a permit for one bull in the South Luangwa National Park, but I've just heard of an old loner whose been causing havoc at villages near Chadiza, close to the Nyasaland border. He's been damaging fences and messing with their crops."

She grasped his arm and tucked it around her. She was shaking. "Why do you think the locals call it the *wakuda kufa?*"

He laughed as he held her tight. "Black death. Nonsense. If that old one is still around by the end of May, we'll be doing the villagers a favor. We'll stop his rampage and their nightmare."

He pulled her on top of him and slid his hands down her back. Her shivering ceased as her breasts pressed through her thin nightgown against his chest.

"I still don't want you to go, *Bwana* Ferreira," Maria murmured. She leaned in and kissed him. *It's been too long.*

Louis sighed as he returned her kisses. "I've *never* prepared this hard for a hunt. *Never.* I want you to stop worrying." His kisses became more demanding as he pulled her bottom tightly against his pelvis.

# 6

*The hunters make final preparations. May 1962*

Years later, Louis Ferreira would ask himself why they had decided to go during the last weekend of May in late fall. At the time, he had thought of many reasons. He also had difficulty recalling the first sign that the blossoming camaraderie between him and Phil Vermeulen was under duress.

Hunting in the fall, with winter around the corner, made the sun more forgiving. On a good summer's day, temperatures could reach 112 in the shade. Finding and tracking a buffalo could take a day, if not two. At some point, a hunter always had to leave the vehicles behind and go on foot. It stood to reason: May was the better choice.

Louis had grown to love the autumnal reds, yellows, and browns of the falling *mopani* leaves. The Luangwa Valley then turned into a color palette. Tiring of its beauty was impossible. But there was no question that hunting during the rainy season brought scant joy. The rains always started in November and often turned vast stretches of the savannah into marshes. Going now, with less foliage on the trees and underbrush, would force Mr. Buffalo to work much harder to hide.

It never ceased to amaze Louis how a two-thousand-pound animal standing five feet six at the shoulders could play hide and seek with its pursuers. The colossal beast had little trouble disappearing as soon as it sensed pursuit. It was a master escape artist.

Two Chevy trucks, their truck beds covered with canvas canopies, and packed for a three-day safari, left Katete station an hour before sunrise. Driving his own truck, Phil took the lead. Louis and Charles Chombe accompanied him, each man comfortable enough on the long one-piece seat. Ulrich Wessels and Kobus Kok followed in the second truck. They were driving to meet Pemba Chiluba, their official tracker, at their first campsite inside the Luangwa park. Pemba had gone ahead the previous day to scout for the whereabouts of a potential bovine candidate.

Two weeks earlier, the wandering lone bull (which had become a nuisance in the Chadiza district) had been killed by local police. Its death was necessary after the buffalo had attacked an elderly man and sent him to the hospital, guaranteeing that he'd spend his remaining years in a wheelchair.

Louis struggled to shake his unease. He was unfamiliar with having the jitters before a hunt, but a strange feeling pushed up in his throat. He had no doubt that they were ready. *We've trained and prepared so hard for this hunt.* He leaned sideways for a better look at his friend, Phil. Charles sat between them, half-asleep with folded arms, legs planted wide, and head nodding. Phil, lost in thought, concentrated as he navigated the neglected road surface. Progress was slow.

Louis recalled their conversation from the previous evening. Phil had phoned him after supper. He had sounded distant, almost embarrassed.

"Louis, do you think the others will have a problem if Rianna came along?"

Louis's brow furrowed as he recalled his reaction. Everybody knew who Phil's daughter was. Louis dropped the receiver but grabbed it before it crashed to the floor.

"Phil?" *Had the man stopped taking his malaria pills?* "We're not going *camping*. Isn't she only *eleven*?" Louis remembered the tall, self-assured redhead standing next to her dad at the shooting range. She had attended their last four practices. She had even convinced her father to let her shoot. Louis had been surprised, as had everyone else there, about how well-placed her shots were, all grouped close together inside the target. *Who'd taught her that?*

Phil coughed several times before he continued. "Rianna's almost *twelve*. She's as tall as her mother. And she's fit. She scales mango trees. None of the boys and few of the men can keep up with her."

Which was true enough. Louis had heard the *Chinyanjas* talk about the Vermeulen girl who climbed the notorious big mango tree, her favorite, in Katete. *But damn it!*

Louis sighed. "Does this carry Anna's blessing?"

"If *you* say yes, Anna will let her come."

*Oh, dear Lord, now I have to make the decision! What has Missions done to us? Have we all lost our common sense? It's bad enough that the Chichewas want to chase the British into the Nyasa Lake since the Indian Ocean is too far. They're fed up with the Colonialists. What is happening to us, the Amissioni?*

"Phil," he answered, after catching his breath. "Let me phone the others. I'll let you know."

*What did the poor girl's parents think? Taking an eleven-year-old girl along with six adult males in the middle of the African bush on a buffalo hunt? Dr. Rossouw, the Missions' Secretary, will suffer a stroke if he finds out.*

After that call, Louis had immediately phoned Wessels and Kok. Both men were as shocked and surprised at the request.

It was a unanimous no.

He called Phil only after going for a brisk walk outside to clear his head. Try as he might, he could not find a single good reason to take the girl along.

"Sorry, Phil. I spoke to both Ulrich and Kobus. She *has* to stay home."

As Phil sighed deeply and ended their call, Louis heard the roaring waters of the Falls from years ago, when he had gone looking for Phil along its slippery stairs.

Now, he caught Phil's eye as he swerved to avoid a pothole, waking the snoring Charles. *I hope he isn't still mad at me for preventing the shiny red apple of his eye from coming along.*

Charles laughed as he rubbed his face to hide his embarrassment. "*Moni, bwanas*! Did I fall asleep? Did I snore?"

Louis laughed and patted him on the back. "Has someone been gallivanting through the night, Mr. Chombe?"

Charles shook his head. "Not true, *bwana*. I'll be awake when the sun sits *there*." He indicated a spot above the horizon. "This is too early for me."

———

By ten that morning, the two vehicles reached the camp where Pemba Chiluba awaited them. Long before the vehicles came to a standstill, it was obvious that the tracker had great news. He paced up and down under the *baobab* tree like a lion in captivity. When the first truck reached him, the one in which Charles Chombe was traveling, Pemba lurched forward and yanked the door open, unable to wait any longer.

"*Moni, Mbusa! Moni, bwana!*"

He turned to Charles and jabbered fast in *Chinyanja*, taking hold of his arm and pulling him aside. He spoke too fast for the *Amissioni* to follow. They had all gathered by now in a semi-circle around the excited tracker and his friend.

The bush around them was alive with the incessant cicadas' songs, interrupted only by an occasional birdcall and anxious yelping from a troop of baboons that loitered on the outskirts of the campground. The earth was steaming and the sun wasn't at its peak yet. The smell of red earth and dead leaves hung around the men.

Pemba kept repeating "*njati*" and "*njanji*": buffalo and tracks. He demonstrated with his curved hands for the men to see. The tracks were big and fresh.

He turned to Louis Ferreira. "*Inde, bwana*! This bull is a *migolomigolo*. He's massive."

"How *far* from here, Pemba?" Louis asked.

The tracker laughed, embarrassed. "It take Pemba one hour. Two for the *bwanas*—if I come with you."

Louis nodded. The man's response held no menace. He had stated a simple fact: he was a tracker used to the bush and they were not.

"How fresh?"

Pemba glanced at the glaring sky then shaded his eyes. The sun promised to be unforgiving by midday. He held up three fingers. "Three hours, *bwana*."

Louis turned toward the group. "Shall we first unpack and set up camp? Or grab a bite to eat and be ready in fifteen minutes, then leave everything on the vehicles and follow Pemba?"

The men deliberated. Kobus Kok was the only one who felt they should rather pitch camp and then reconsider.

Louis turned toward Charles. This is not what he had prepared for, to sit in the shade of this forest giant on his camping stool, sipping coffee. "What do *you* think? And what does *Pemba* recommend?"

The two *Chinyanjas* had another heated discussion. Pemba, glancing at the men, couldn't believe the *Amissioni* had seconds thoughts. As far as he was concerned, they should have been on their way an hour ago. He had located the *migolomigolo*!

Louis thanked the slender tracker for his trouble and reassured him that they were in agreement—now was the best time. They'd have a light meal and be ready to go. They'd set up camp in the afternoon when they got back. The *Chichewa's* face broke into a grin—there was hope.

Louis addressed the group. "Gentlemen, have some sandwiches. Fill your water bottles and get your rifles ready. We're leaving in *fifteen*."

They had five rifles between them. Each man would carry ten rounds. Pemba was happy to carry only three carved sticks with him, which could be used as a makeshift tripod to stabilize a rifle's barrel.

Louis followed Phil to his truck to get the items from the vehicle. They unclipped the canvas flaps at the back. As they dropped the tailgate with a bang, movement inside the back of the truck made Louis duck sideways. *Good Lord! Somebody's inside the truck!*

"*Hello*, Daddy! *Hello,* Uncle Louis!" Rianna Vermeulen called out as she jumped from the truck bed, shook her mop of red hair, and stretched her limbs. She glanced at the two men. Her eyes asked, "What's wrong?"

Phil seemed as astonished as his colleague. "Rianna! *What's* this? I told you last night you couldn't come along!"

She laughed. "Don't be mad, Daddy. I *did* ask. I've heard what Pemba told you about the *migolomigolo* bull that he's tracked down. I will keep up with—"

"You will do *nothing* of the kind, young lady!" Louis Ferreira had recovered and stepped closer toward the self-assured teenager, who suddenly looked less certain of herself. She scuttled closer toward her father.

Louis spun toward Phil. "I thought I made it clear to you last night? Rianna was *not* to come along! Why did you allow her to sneak into your truck under the protection of dark—"

Phil put his arm around his daughter's shoulders. He pulled himself erect, jutting his chin. His jaw twitched. "She did *not* do it with my blessing, Louis! No one could see a thing when we left."

"Well, then you'll have to unpack your truck's contents, leave the stuff behind for us, and take her back. We have to get going. You know what Pemba reported. That bull is moving."

Phil gave his daughter's shoulders a quick squeeze and stepped forward. "Sorry, Louis, but I'm not doing that. She can come along, and I'm going *with* you guys."

"Phil."

"I've practiced as hard as any of you for this hunt!"

"Rianna's presence has changed *everything!*"

"Let's hear what the others think."

A new circle had formed around the redhead, her father, and Louis Ferreira. Everyone voiced their opinions in urgent and upset tones, airing their surprise and annoyance with the audacity of the young girl to have snuck onto the truck early that morning.

Louis held up his hands. "Guys! Gentlemen! Here's the situation: This young lady, this stowaway, *cannot* go along. The hunt is taking place as planned. Her father has to take her back."

He looked the men in the eyes, one after the other. "Show of hands. Who says she goes back?"

Phil scowled. Rianna's dark eyes bore right through him.

Ulrich Wessels and Kobus Kok's hands shot up.

"Charles? Pemba?" Louis looked at the *Chinyanja* men whose hands remained at their sides. He shook his head.

Charles Chombe and Pemba Chiluba pulled up their shoulders. They were embarrassed, but they were also aware of the praise going around for the long-legged redhead, the renowned mango tree-climber. They had also heard how well-placed her shots were.

Charles muttered, "*Bwana.*"

Louis spun back toward Rianna's father. "You realize what the Old Man in Lusaka will do with us if *anything* happens to your girl?"

"It's ultimately *my* responsibility, as her father."

"Yes, but the Old Man will demand *my* head."

Phil chuckled. "I thought he'd be more lenient toward a fellow *Afrikaner Broederbond* man."

Louis clenched his fists as he stepped closer to his friend. Through gritted teeth he said for his friend's ears only, "*Stop* it, Phil! I belonged to the AB as a student. They have no jurisdiction here in the bush. I can't speak for the boss."

"That's not what I've heard. Dr. Rossouw is well-connected—"

"*Phil!* The issue here is Rianna. We have to come to a workable agreement."

Rianna, clinging to her father's arm, jumped with excitement. "Oh, thank you, Uncle Louis! I will stay at the back, with Daddy. I won't be any—" Her dark eyes shone with the same intensity she had when their families visited the Falls.

"I have *not* given my permission, Missy!" Louis stomped off to the side, motioning Ulrich and Kobus to follow him. More deliberation followed.

Louis turned back. "Phil, does her mother—does Anna know?"

Phil shook his head and glanced at his daughter. She cast her eyes down, shrugged her shoulders, and mumbled to herself.

"Did you *tell* your mother?" Phil took a step toward his daughter.

"No, Daddy," Rianna whispered, sounding for the first time like the eleven-year-old she was. She swallowed, then added, "But I left her *a note*. On my bed. She knows by now I'm with you."

"This is *dangerous*."

"Not more than climbing thirty feet to my lookout branch in my mango tree every day."

"Rianna."

"*Pappie, 'seblief.*" Her eyes brimmed with moisture. Her lower lip trembled.

Louis cleared his throat. *Look at the time. This silly girl.* "Gentlemen? Phil?" He scanned the group's faces. "Have we reached a consensus?"

"Ulrich?" Louis received a shrug.

"Kobus?" Another shrug of non-commitment.

Charles and Pemba laughed. They had no squabbles with the *mtsikana* coming along. She could run fast, she could climb trees better than any of them, and she could even shoot. She had snuck in the dark into the back of an old truck, so she embraces fear. Hell, what *more* do the *Amissioni* want from a person?

"*Bwana* . . . If we want to catch bull, we stop talking now," Pemba said. He gestured at the sky. "Look, the sun." It was time, his eyes said.

Rianna scrambled onto the truck bed and disappeared. When she jumped down, she hollered, "See, Uncle Louis, I came prepared." She held up high her water bottle, binoculars, a sturdy walking stick, and a shoulder knapsack.

It was Louis Ferreira's turn to roll his eyes.

*Women!*

# 7

## Tracking the beast

Pemba, armed with his three thin sticks, a water bottle, and binoculars, took the lead.

Next followed Kobus Kok, Louis, and Charles Chombe. Behind them came Phil and his daughter. Ulrich Wessels formed the rearguard, his "buffalo rifle" hanging from his shoulder. Depending on the terrain and vegetation, the group stuck to this loose formation as they wandered deeper into the park. In narrower spots they were forced to go single file.

Shade was in short supply. The *mopanis* had shed their leaves, decorating the bush and forest floor with reds and yellows. Pemba was on a mission—he kept a steady pace. They were soon drenched, their clothes glued to their skin, and above them the seething sky remained blinding white. The route led them past many savannah animals, and each time Pemba spotted them he'd freeze, the hand with the sticks held high, the other hand pointing where to look. They passed scores of impalas that disappeared behind the tall grass. They only got a glimpse of the bushbuck. When the group came too close for their liking, three giraffes took off in the opposite direction.

It took an hour of focused walking for Pemba to find his marker: a strip of yellow cloth tied to a small branch. He gave a happy cry when he found the original spoor.

Rianna gasped when the aroma of buffalo dung hit them. The scorching sun, dozens of dung beetles, and legions of flies had all worked hard to engulf them with a pungent smell that burnt nostrils, made eyes tear up, and caused them to question the sanity of the exercise. She swatted at the insects, dug in her shoulder bag, pulled out a black bandanna, and tied it over her nose. She looked like an extra from a cowboy film. She gritted her teeth and said nothing. *I'll show these men—all of them, and Uncle Louis in particular—I'm not a baby anymore. I'm not a silly little girl. Climbing trees isn't the only thing I can do well.*

The only living creatures able to keep up with the midday sun and boiling heat without flinching were the cicadas. And the dung beetles. *Do they never tire? Do they never sleep?*

Pemba, having sensed the discomfort of his now-haphazard hunting party, beckoned them closer as they scaled a rocky outcrop. "*Mtengo, bwana.*"

*Trees.* Trees with leaves meant *shade*. No one required a second invitation to scamper for a cool spot.

Rianna found refuge under a *mopani* with all its foliage still in place. She rolled her bandanna into a narrow band and tied it around her head, pulling her matted hair away from her sunburnt face.

Pemba beamed at them. "We eat. We drink water. We rest. *Inde?*"

Everyone laughed and cheered the tracker. Of the seven in the group, Pemba was the only one who seemed to have only gone for a five-minute stroll in the veld. He seemed fresh and unscathed. He remained standing as he nibbled on cooked maize porridge from his knapsack.

"How far ahead is the bull?" Louis asked.

Pemba cocked his head. "One hour, *bwana.*" He chuckled. "The bull is lazy. He traveled fast this morning. He takes many rests now. We hurry—we catch him. *Inde?*"

"*Inde*, Pemba." Louis said. *Yes, we will certainly catch him.*

———

Rianna ambled over to her father. He sat on a fallen tree trunk, his back against a rock-face that was part of the outcrop they sat upon. His eyes were closed. She settled down a few feet away and started braiding her damp hair while watching him.

Phil's eyes flew open. "What?" His face softened as he smiled at her. *You look so much like your mother, dearest child. You are so brave*, his eyes said.

She smiled, then took a deep breath. "Daddy, are you and Uncle Louis still *friends?*"

"We *are.*"

"Then why are you so angry with him? Mommy said you have made peace."

"We have."

"And me being here today doesn't help?"

He laughed, avoiding her eyes.

"Being a grown up is hard, sometimes."

"I'm sorry that I messed up. But being a *child* is hard!" Rianna called out. "I'm in trouble all of the time. I'm not a *kleintjie* anymore, but you adults treat me like a baby!"

"Rianna, you're eleven."

"Almost twelve!" She pushed out her chest. "I'm growing up. I've asked mother to make me my first training bra, Daddy."

Crimson crept up his face. "Rianna! I don't think this is—"

"Gentlemen! Rianna! Time to go!" Louis called out. He stood next to Pemba. They were both ready. "Everybody check their weapons. One round in the chamber. Safeties on." He clapped his hands. "Let's go, guys!"

Pemba trotted ahead, knelt down in the tall grass, and clambered on the last boulder as they descended the outcrop. He pointed east with his pale white sticks. "*Bwana*, the *njati*, the buffalo turn, he go east now. Come—we have rest, now we go fast. *Inde?*"

"*Inde*, Pemba!" Rianna called out as she ran ahead of her father and the men and fell in next to the tracker. He laughed and smiled at the redhead who had little trouble keeping up with him.

Soon he showed her what he was looking for. Each time he paused, bent forward, or spotted a dropping, a spoor, or disturbance left by the animal, he explained what he was inspecting in great detail. He pointed out the difference between the imprints of the animal's front and rear hooves. The front hooves' imprints were much larger and deeper because of the extra weight the animal carried in its front and upper part of its body.

He chuckled. "The *njati* think he is alone," he confided once they had reached the bottom of the hill and had once again changed direction.

"The bull doesn't *know* we're following him, Pemba?" Rianna's eyes were large as she glanced around at the surrounding bush. She was still startled when a rasp of guinea fowl scuttled into the underbrush with their shrill *tjirr-tje-tje-tjirr*.

Pemba confirmed her question. "*Iyayi*. He do not know. He take his time."

Behind them, the formal grouping had become unstitched. Many of the men had lowered their guard. The only person still in his original position was Ulrich Wessels with the .416 Rigby. His instruction had been clear to form the rearguard, and he intended on doing just that.

Phil Vermeulen fell in pace with Louis Ferreira. The men were quiet as if sizing up one another. They cherished the cease-fire. Both kept an eye on the tracker and his latest fan, the redhead, who were equal in size and height and kept going at a similar steady pace out front. To the uninitiated eye, it seemed as if the young *Amissioni* girl had missed her calling. She seemed a natural apprentice-tracker.

Her father grinned with pride. His friend scoffed.

The scouting pair scanned the bush from side to side and paused from time to time when Pemba held his three sticks high, or when he bent down because the spoor had become too feeble to follow. Then Pemba would scuttle forward again, picking up speed, and their pursuit resumed.

"You have a remarkable child," Louis said as they witnessed how Rianna was just as quick as Pemba to hold up her stick when she spotted antelope and game crossing their party's path. Louis turned toward his friend and chuckled, thinking, *It's often not easy to admit our deficiencies to our fellow men.*

Phil laughed as he watched his daughter trot ahead next to Pemba, her excitement on display. "She takes after her mother."

"She was a spirited young girl then, when our families visited the Falls, but she's grown into an even stronger-minded young woman," Louis said. "Seems I was wrong about her."

"It's the first time she has disobeyed me like this. I'm sorry if I came across as unreasonable."

Louis shrugged his shoulders as he repositioned the rifle strap. "Likewise."

"I think *Anna* had a heart attack when she discovered Rianna's note this morning—never mind the Old Man in Lusaka."

The group froze in their tracks—both Pemba and Rianna had their sticks held high. Rianna had turned toward her father, pointing to their far left. "Daddy, *look*," she whispered. Fifty yards away, a black sable bull faced them in the shade of an acacia. It snorted, shook its head with its majestic curved horns, then turned and trotted away with confidence—a real show-off.

Pemba lowered his white sticks and the group moved forward again.

"Why do you have such an issue with the *Afrikaner Broederbond*?" Louis asked, glancing sideways at his friend. "Don't you think it's improbable believing they have a say in what is happening to us here in the bush?"

"No, I don't. They're like *this* with the church, the DRC, that sent us out."

Phil held his thumb and index finger an inch apart.

Louis chuckled, shrugging his shoulders. "They're a cultural organization. They've been around for forty years. It was born in the aftermath following the Anglo-Boer war."

Phil shook his head. "You give the AB too little credit. It's a powerful organization. It dictates what happens to you and—"

"Do you *believe* that? This is Northern Rhodesia!"

"I do!"

"Bogus." Louis snorted as he hastened his pace to keep up with the tracker.

"Old Man Rossouw is very cozy with the AB bosses."

"Bullshit." Louis's voice had climbed an octave.

"Why do you think I am sucking at the hind teat, my friend, if not for the AB? I've never been one of the inner circle."

"There are only so many positions open in the Field. It's an internal arrangement by Missions. You knew that when you started out."

Philip argued back. "Yes, but behind the scenes, many strings are pulled . . . by people—by human beings—human hands. Humans like the *Oubaas* in Lusaka, and the AB's inner circle. It's so convenient for the church to justify its actions by proclaiming, 'It's the hand of God,' but in the meantime, it's the hand of man!"

"Now you're going too far! That's close to blasphemy!" Louis said, his voice rising.

"Much of what the church does is a front."

"A front for *what*? You're implying I'm being privileged *above* you! Being the *Oubaas's witbroodjie*?"

"You *are* his favored pet!" Phil called out.

"How *dare* you!"

The two men had stopped walking. They faced one another, their knuckles white as they clasped their .375 rifles. Still, the barrels pointed at the grass at their feet.

Pemba and Rianna were calling from the front.

Behind them, Ulrich Wessels had closed the gap between them. The two hotheads needed a time-out, like boys on the playground. Ulrich lurched forward and grasped each man by the shoulder. "*Stop it*, you idiots!" He hissed under his breath, "There are two *Chinyanjas* and an eleven-year-old girl up there. What kind of example are you two setting? Stop this *instant!*" He yanked the two perplexed men toward him, their faces inches apart. "If you two had been paying *any* attention, you'd have heard your tracker's warning. We are *this far* from that bull. Pemba and Rianna have come upon warm dung. It's minutes old. The people could hear the two of you bitching like old wives on the *other side* of the Luangwa valley. So shut *the hell up!*" Ulrich shoved them apart and away from him.

Both men gawked at Ulrich. They had never heard him speak like that.

"Daddy?" Rianna called again, lowering her voice. She took her father by the arm and pulled him away.

"*Bwana!* Come look. *Njati*." Pemba had also run closer to get Louis. He took the now enraged missionary by the elbow and led him to the latest fresh dropping.

The tracker bent closer to the ground, kneeled, jumped up again, and glanced at the sky. He didn't need a wristwatch to tell what time it was. He turned to Louis. "*Bwana*, in three hours it will be dark."

"Could you see him?" Louis whispered.

The *Chinyanja* shook his head no. "*Iyayi*."

"Which way is the wind coming? Can he smell us?" Louis asked.

Ulrich murmured. "No, but he could hear the two of you *screaming* at each other."

Pemba again shook his head and pointed at a cluster of trees half a mile away. "We will find the *njati* in there."

"How do you know he's there?" Louis asked.

The tracker tapped his chest. "My heart tells me." He grinned. "And my eyes."

"Thank you, Pemba."

"The *bwana* thank me after we shoot him, *inde*?"

Louis Ferreira cleared his throat, pushed his hand through his matted hair, and faced Phil. "I'm sorry that I've been such an asshole."

Phil shrugged his shoulders then murmured an inaudible apology.

Louis turned toward the rest of the group. "Okay, everybody! Check your rifles again. One round in the chamber. Safeties on. Have your other rounds at hand. Pemba, you go in the front with Kobus. Charles and I will go next, then it's Phil and Rianna, and Ulrich is our rearguard." He tried his best to grin. "Let's go."

Pemba led the hunting party toward the cluster of trees along the forest's border. They changed course once when the wind changed direction.

Three hundred yards from the cluster of trees, Pemba dropped to his knee and crouched down. He studied the animal through his binoculars. The men and Rianna followed his example. He turned toward Louis. "*Bwana,* see the *njati*? He is *migolomigolo.*"

Louis clasped his binoculars. He whistled. "He *is* massive. He must be twenty-two hundred pounds!"

Next to him Rianna whispered, "*Migolomigolo.*"

# 8

## *The buffalo*

Pemba led them, this time single file, sticking to the edge of the forest within the tree line. They would stop at a hundred yards. The goal was to get to fifty yards for a better shot.

No one said a word.

Pemba slowly held up his hand, now without the sticks. He didn't wish to alert the bull. He went down on his haunches. The others followed. He held up ten fingers, crossed his index fingers, and showed them ten fingers again—they were at one hundred yards. He tested the wind. He pointed at Louis, Charles, and Kobus. *Follow me*, his eyes said. They'd have to approach from yet another angle. The wind was playing games.

Phil, Rianna, and Ulrich would remain in that spot.

It was as if the cicadas held their breaths, or they must have grown tired of their monotonous wing-song. In the distance, the barking of a troop of baboons faded as the animals scattered deeper into the forest. The moment the party paused, flies joined their ranks. The midday heat had eased off, but perspiration still framed each hunter's face. The smell of the veld with its long grass, fallen leaves, and animal dung was only overshadowed by the odor from their sweating bodies.

Louis, suddenly aware of the gravity of the situation, approached the three staying behind. He grasped Ulrich's hand and shook it, lowering his voice. "Thank you . . . for keeping an eye over all of us." He lowered his eyes for a moment and cleared his throat. "And . . . thank you for bringing us to our senses . . . back there." He pointed at Phil and himself.

Ulrich held his hand, forcing eye contact. "Be *careful*." He let go and added, "I'll keep my eyes open."

Louis turned toward Phil and his daughter. "Rianna, I was wrong about you. Seems to me Pemba has found himself a new apprentice?"

She grinned at him, clinging to her father's arm, making her appear all of her eleven years. "Oh, I loved taking the spoor with Pemba, Uncle Louis!"

"Phil, keep an eye on her." The two men shook hands.

The next moment Phil pulled his arm free from Rianna's grip and steered Louis to the side. "I've been thinking. I shouldn't have to stay behind under the trees, watching."

Louis snapped his arm free. "What do you mean?"

"Why are you *punishing* me?" Phil asked.

Louis Ferreira cocked his brow. He said nothing.

Phil stepped up close to his friend. "There's *one* buffalo. Both of us want to shoot him. Why *you*?"

Louis scoffed. "She's your daughter—her presence has changed everything. Someone has to babysit her."

"Ulrich has his four-sixteen. She'll be fine with him."

"She'll be *fine*?" Louis's voice climbed.

"*Bwana*," Pemba whispered a warning.

"I'm sorry, Phil, but I cannot allow that. She has to stay, and you are her father. It's for her own safety!"

Behind them, Pemba cleared his throat. His voice remained soft. "*Bwana*, hurry. The bull is moving."

Phil stepped forward. "I'm coming *with* you guys."

Louis placed his hand on Phil's chest. "You will *not*! You'll stay behind with Rianna and Ulrich. This is an *order*!"

Phil sneered, "Hah! You're not my boss because you're the *Oubaas's witbroodjie* and an AB confidante!"

"You're a bloody *liar!*" With his rifle held in front of him like a ramming rod, Louis shoved his friend backward with it.

"Daddy!" Rianna dashed closer, pushed the barrel of her father's rifle toward the ground, and hugged him the moment Ulrich pulled the two men apart.

His eyes shot fire. "*Louis Ferreira*! Do you want me to take your rifle? Then Kobus can shoot the bloody buffalo!"

Pemba's voice was urgent now. "*Bwanas!* The *njati* is running!" He spun around, not waiting for an answer, and jogged in the direction of Charles and Kobus.

Ulrich grabbed Louis by the sleeve and pulled him in the direction Pemba had run. "You'd better run, *before* I change my mind. Don't force me to make a citizen's arrest!"

Phil tried to pull free from Rianna clasping his arm to get past Ulrich. "The *bastard*. Rianna, let go of me!"

"Daddy, no!"

"Phil, cut it out!" Ulrich stepped in front of the upset man and took hold of the barrel of his .375. A short struggle followed.

"Idiot!" Ulrich hissed under his breath. "For the sake of Rianna!"

"He *assaulted* me!"

"Spare me the theatrics, Vermeulen. He's right. You *have* Rianna to think about."

"Bloody *Broederbonder*," Phil sneered as he pulled himself free and plopped down on a fallen tree that stood chair-high.

———

When Louis caught up with Pemba and the men, his breathing was fast and his heart raced—not because he was unfit, but because he seethed. He felt light-headed. *Dear Lord, Phil is my friend! But he was out of line! It's his brat of a daughter who's been responsible for all this drama.*

Pemba had his binoculars to his eyes. He glanced at Louis and clicked with his tongue.

"What?" Louis asked.

"The *njati* is clever. I do not see him. You and other *bwana* made much noise. *Inde?*" He clicked again. "He runs. Now we have to run hard to catch him." Then he pointed at the sky. "Or night will catch us if we talk too much."

Louis realized this was the closest the shy tracker would come to reprimanding him in public. Pemba was definitely not of the opinion that Rianna was responsible for all the drama. Louis made peace with staying at the back of the group once he noticed glances from Kobus and Charles. They jogged single file behind the clearly upset Pemba. The tracker had taken off without verifying that the others were following.

The hunters reached the cluster of trees where the buffalo had grazed right before the altercation between Louis and Phil.

Pemba held up his hand with the sticks, then knelt down. When he straightened up, his binoculars were in position. "The *njati* know we look for him. We hurry. He go fast."

Louis caught up with the tracker. "Will you be able to find the place where we left the other *bwanas* and the *mtsikana*?"

"*Inde*. I know the Luangwa park." He had slowed their pace down to a walk.

The trees had grown scarcer. Of the buffalo, there was no sign.

"Where *is* he, Pemba?"

"He is *mzimu*." Pemba shrugged his shoulders.

Louis chuckled. "He is *not* a ghost. Nonsense."

"Pemba know the park. *Njati* know park better. *Njati* know hiding places."

"Have you *lost* him?"

Pemba shook his head, pointing at a fresh hoof imprint in the soft sand. He scanned ahead, brought his binoculars to his eyes, and mumbled, "Trees. Three hundred yard."

He faced Louis as they walked. "*Bwana*, you shoot *njati* before?"

Louis beamed. "Yes. Four years ago—single shot—through the shoulder and the heart."

"Four years is long time. Pemba see *bwana* forget no noise."

The smile on Louis's face faded.

Pemba froze and held his hand with the sticks up high. He whispered, "This *njati* have good ears. He turn, he move closer. Now only two hundred yard."

Louis paused and turned to the other men. "Check your rifles, gentlemen. One round in the chamber. Safeties off. Make sure your other rounds won't get stuck in your belts."

———

Charles turned toward Louis. He'd said few words since they'd left the vehicles that morning. He knew his place—his country hadn't won its independence from the British Crown yet. But he feared that Louis wasn't in the right state of mind for such a hunt.

"*Bwana*, it was impossible not to listen to the arguments between you and *Bwana* Phil. I can see you are still upset. This bull is a *migolomigolo*. He is also angry—that's why he turned around. He has good ears. He is dangerous." Charles cleared his throat. "Forgive me, *bwana*. We need a steady hand . . . Will you be able to shoot?"

Louis's face turned crimson. His knuckles were blanched as he brandished his .375 H&H. "I *am* ready!" He took a step toward Charles.

The Kitchen Boy from *Madzi Moyo* stood his ground, his arm with the rifle relaxed at his side. It was impossible to read his face.

Pemba's urgent whisper brought them back. "*No* more talk, *bwana*. Silence, Charles. You all come *now*."

Pemba and Louis remained five steps ahead of Kobus and Charles. The men had their rifles in their hands pointing outward as they advanced. Their eyes scanned the bush as they carefully placed each boot. The red and yellow leaves underfoot made more noise than the grass.

Pemba's observation that the buffalo knew the park better seemed to be prophetic. The trees in the area where the bull had led them to now still had most of their leaves. Even the underbrush had sidestepped fall—its foliage was lush. Incessant cicadas' songs and innumerable flies followed them step-by-step. It was wiser to tolerate and not swat at the insects. Unnecessary movement could alert the beast, and they were too close. He might sense the slightest movement.

Pemba held up his hand and then pointed at two o'clock.

Louis sucked in his breath. Instinct kicked in. He brought his rifle to his shoulder. Through a narrow clearing between the trees, between trunks, bush, and leaves, he saw part of the animal—its head and torso—gigantic.

The bull looked him in the eyes. It challenged him.

*Oh, those magnificent horns!*

It was less than fifty yards away—perhaps only forty.

*What color is the eye of the African savannah buffalo?*

The cicadas held their breaths.

The bull snorted. One hoof kicked up grass.

Louis pulled the .375 into his shoulder, his eye squinting through the telescopic sight. His shaking hands made it impossible to keep the animal's chest in his sight.

"*Bwana?*" Pemba's whisper was almost inaudible.

The bull snorted louder and hit the ground again with a hoof.

"*Bwana, shoot!*"

The bull charged.

A single shot rang out. The bull lurched, swerved to the side, and then disappeared. Pemba had called him the *mzimu*. He was right. The bull *was* a ghost.

"*Come, bwana!* We follow!"

Louis unfroze and followed, but Pemba remained a step ahead of the men until they reached the spot where the bull was shot. The surrounding leaves, grass, and copper sand wore scant blood spatters.

Kobus fidgeted around. It was easy to get the impression *he* had shot the animal. "I saw how he jumped, Louis! You *got* him!"

Louis shook his head. His lips were pursed. "I'm afraid I've only nicked him."

Charles's impassive face said what he thought.

"Is there a *blood trail*, Pemba?" Louis asked, fighting to slow his breathing down. He felt dizzy. He had to know.

"*Chepa.*"

*Only a little!* thought Louis. *Damn. Then I've only hurt the bastard. Now he'll be really mad—pissed off and dangerous.*

Louis struggled to get a new round into the chamber. "Go ahead Pemba . . . Please . . . We need to *find* him." He glanced at the sky. The shadows had become taller.

Pemba followed his gaze. He clicked with his tongue. The sun was in a hurry.

Charles called from fifteen feet away. "Pemba. *Bwanas*. Over *here!*" He scanned the bush around them, keeping his rifle at the ready, before bending over and pointing at blood spatters leading in the direction from where they had come. Kobus noticed Charles's stance and followed his example: he'd stand guard while the others inspected the spoor. *Who knows what the bull's up to now?*

Pemba looked at his friend Charles and clicked again. They rapidly chattered in *Chichewa*. Pemba pointed with his sticks and turned toward Louis. "*Bwana, njati* go where we leave *bwanas* and *mtsikana, inde?*"

Charles added, "It's clear he's wounded, but he's not losing much blood."

"He could be bleeding *internally*," piped Kobus.

Pemba and Charles shrugged their shoulders. The bull had moved too fast and had disappeared too quickly to be in serious peril.

The *Chinyanjas*' body language made their thoughts clear: *you Amissioni from the South think you know the bush and its creatures. Think again, bwanas.*

Louis stepped closer. He had his breathing under control. "Lead the way, Pemba. Gentlemen: diamond formation. Keep your rifles pointing outward. The bull's hurt, he's mad, and he may turn *back* on us."

## 9

## *A wounded buffalo*

"Daddy, Uncle Louis *shot* him!" Rianna called out. She'd heard the single shot ring out over the valley. Birds scattered and took flight from the surrounding bush. Cicadas fell silent, but only for a moment. Ulrich and Phil both snapped out of their semi-slumbering states under the *mopani*. They had found comfortable spots underneath the old tree, which had retained most of its leaves, giving them a reprieve from the afternoon heat. They joined Rianna who danced around them, blabbering about the hero's welcome they would receive at Katete when they returned with the slain buffalo.

"All we know is *one* shot has been fired," her father said.

"Oh, Daddy! You're such a spoilsport." She hooked in at his elbow and tried to make him dance with her in the clearing within the tall grass.

Ulrich checked his rifle and glanced at Phil. "Safety off, my friend. I don't trust that *migolomigolo*." He turned to Rianna and grinned. "Don't sell your chickens, Missy. Not yet."

"Agh, Uncle Ulrich! Come dance with me."

Ulrich handed his rifle to Phil and humored the enthused redhead with the black bandanna tied around her head, which made her look like a bandit leader. He hooked in and completed three fast twirls, spinning her out far and wide. She shrieked with glee.

While she gathered herself and regained her balance, he took his rifle from her father and slipped the safety off again. "Rianna—listen my dear. Your father was right. Until we get confirmation or see the dead carcass, we have to remain vigilant."

"But why?"

"The *Chinyanjas* call him *wamasiye wolenga,* the widow-maker—with good reason."

"But Daddy said one three-seventy-five round can kill an African buffalo."

"It certainly can—if it strikes him through the heart or center of his chest. They are notorious for ambushing their pursuers."

She brandished her walking stick, stepped closer to her father, and glanced at the bush around them. "How do we stop the buffalo from surprising us?"

"We stay one step ahead of him. No more lying under the tree. We stand watch. Keep our eyes and ears open."

"Daddy, then we have to find a spot with less trees and bush, where it's more open. Where we can *see* him before he *sneaks* up on us." She shivered as she leaned against her father and clung to his arm.

The men glanced at each other over her head and nodded in agreement.

Phil chuckled as they gathered their knapsacks from under the tree. "I'm so proud of you, Honey. Pemba will be too. He'll say you think like a *wosaka*."

Rianna smiled. *I do think like a hunter.*

———

Pemba's hand shot up. Everybody froze midstride. He cupped his ear as if to say, *Listen people.*

They heard the beast before they saw anything. The bush behind them shattered and snapped as the two-tonner stormed their way. The underbrush parted like the Red Sea.

"*Jesu! Bwanas!*"

Two shots were fired.

The buffalo snorted as one round struck him. He gave an explosive growl, dipped his head, and raced at Pemba while swooping low with his horns for the kill. The tracker stood his ground and hollered in *Chinyanja*. He rained his three sticks at the beast's snout. The bull swerved yet again, but as he brushed past the tracker the *migolomigolo's* momentum knocked Pemba to the ground. The man went down with a yell in a cloud of dust. The bushes closed behind the animal just as they had opened, like the waters that had drowned Pharaoh and his cavalry. The ghost vanished.

Kobus shook his head as he glanced at his rifle. *What happened? Did my gun misfire?*

"Pemba!" Charles dropped to his knees in the sienna sand next to his friend. He could see how his own bullet had struck the beast. *Why didn't the monster go down?*

The tracker was covered in a coat of red dirt and dust. He lay motionless. There was no blood on him. *Is his chest moving?*

Louis knelt down on Pemba's other side and grabbed his wrist. "Does he have a pulse?"

The whites of two eyes appeared in the dirt-covered face. Then a smile. *"Moni, bwana."*

The men laughed. They were close to tears. They had all seen the black death speed past.

Pemba sat up and shook his head, glancing from man to man. He turned to Charles. "He is *migolomigolo!*"

"Pemba, can you *move* your legs?" Louis didn't trust the apparent good health of their tracker.

Pemba wiggled his legs, still smiling.

"Nothing broken? No pain? Your breathing doesn't hurt?" Louis insisted. The man who shook his head at him should have been dead.

Charles kneeled forward and put his arm around his friend. "Come. Let's get you up."

Kobus stepped closer, peered into the tracker's eyes, and then glanced at Louis and Charles. "Shall we take him back to where *Bwana* Wessels and Vermeulen are? He might have a concussion."

Pemba and Charles conversed in *Chinyanja.* Charles laughed.

"Shouldn't you carry him on your back, Charles?" Louis asked, glancing at the broad-shouldered African who towered over them.

Pemba chuckled. "*Bwana* think *njati* make me weak? Look, Pemba walk."

The tracker gathered his only white stick that hadn't been shattered and used it as a cane. He stepped forward, then grimaced and gasped, clutching the stick. Charles caught him.

"*Bwana*, take my rifle, please." Charles held his friend upright with one hand and passed his gun to Louis.

"*Where* does it hurt?" Louis leaned closer to the tracker.

Charles went down on his haunches and slipped Pemba onto his back.

Pemba grimaced and said, "*Chichira*" as he pointed to his hip.

Louis slipped his head and shoulders through the strap of Charles's rifle, made it hang behind his back, and took his own rifle in both hands after opening and closing the chamber. He glanced at Kobus. "Safeties off. There's now a clearer blood-spatter trail following the bull, but let's first get back to the others. We have to drop Pemba off. We'll come back. Keep your eyes to that side of the bush."

The shadows were tall. The heat of the day had evaporated as the once-scorching sun cringed toward the horizon.

The tracker's hip may have been hurt, making it impossible for him to walk, but he hadn't lost his situational awareness. He pointed at the sky. "*Bwana* Ferreira, one hour of sun. You take me to where *mtsikana* is. You find *njati*." He patted his friend's shoulder. "Charles help you. He is good tracker, *inde*?"

"*Inde,*" Louis murmured as he scanned the bush on all sides while they retraced their path back to where the others were. He increased his pace, following Pemba's direction. The bush looked the same to him. They would be lost without the slim tracker.

"You kill *njati* before night come, *bwana.*"

"*Inde,* Pemba."

———

"Daddy, did you *hear* that?" The redhead brandished her stick as she'd seen Pemba do.

Phil and Ulrich had both heard. Twigs snapped. Leaves were stepped on. They were on edge, their rifles at the ready. Three shots and two hours later—and no sign of the four. Something was wrong. Something was approaching—something big that didn't care to be discovered.

Then they heard the voices.

"Daddy, it's them!"

"Louis! Is that you?" Ulrich hollered. He sighed as he lowered his rifle.

"Ulrich! Phil! Yes, we're around this little hill."

The four men received a standing ovation as they came into view.

Charles had just slipped Pemba from his back under the big *mopani* when the tracker turned to Louis. "*Bwana,* if night catch you," and he glanced at the horizon and then at Louis's rifle. "From here is one hour to Luwi Bush Camp."

He turned to Charles. "You walk east—fast like me—one hour. You find park road—number five. You go north. Five minutes you see Luwi Camp. *Inde?*"

"*Inde*, my friend. We have to go find that bull before it's dark."

# 10

## To find and kill a wounded buffalo

It took Phil a minute to convince Louis that he wanted to switch places with Kobus. Within half an hour the sun would set, giving them only an hour of light before having to abandon the hunt. Nobody could afford that. The buffalo had to be killed before more people got hurt. Whoever went—would have to run. Walking wasn't an option anymore.

"I'm *fit*, Louis. I can outrun *you*." There was no arrogance in Phil's voice.

Louis's face was drawn. *If I just hadn't messed up that first shot.*

Kobus, a man much smaller in stature than the others, slouched as he listened to the passionate plea.

"Kobus, I'm so sorry, but I *have* to go. We'll have to run all the way." Phil shrugged his shoulders. "That bull needs to be killed *before* dark."

Kobus grinned. "I've had my share. You can go."

Phil spun around, hugged his daughter, and kissed her. "Stay next to Uncle Ulrich, at all times."

"Daddy." Rianna wiped away tears.

Phil hugged her a second time. "I love you. Ulrich will look after you."

Charles cleared his throat. "*Bwanas*! The sun doesn't wait."

The men turned, waved at the four under the *mopani*, and disappeared between the long grass.

Ulrich had undertaken to build a fire in the event that darkness caught up with them, a fire big enough to frighten off any size predator.

After nightfall, the hunter could become the hunted.

———

Charles took the lead. There was nothing to discuss with the two *bwanas*—they had a task to complete. He kept a slow but steady jogging pace. "We'll pick up the blood trail from where the *njati* hit Pemba."

It seemed Louis had found his rhythm. He beamed at Charles as they ran. "*Inde*, Charles!"

Charles grinned at the *bwana* as he navigated the best route to take. The longer shadows made the veld and bush look unfamiliar.

The trio ran in a spear formation, their rifles brandished outward. They were taking a calculated risk. They made more noise running and had less time to look where they stepped and to scan the bush, which would make it easier for the animal to ambush them.

Then again, if they walked with care and kept a lookout every step of the way, they wouldn't make it before sunset.

The men reached the blood-soaked red sand, decorated with two of Pemba's shattered sticks, as the red globe hung above the *baobabs* and *mopanis*. They each took a sip of water, caught their breath, and fanned out to find the bull's most recent trail.

"This way, *bwanas*," Charles called as he found blood spatters leading southeast. It was easier to read this time. The bull was bleeding, and not internally, as Kobus had suggested.

Charles held up a hand. His voice now a whisper, he said, "*Bwanas*, we'll walk fast. No running. Listen for his snorting. Watch where you step. No noise. He can be in hiding."

They moved in a scattered, single-file formation—Charles out front, Louis to the left, with Phil to the right at the back. The shadows between the trees and bush became deeper, darker, larger. Shape, size, and form blurred. Any one of the shadows could be the wounded beast.

The bull must have bolted when shot the second time, mad with pain and in a frenzy. As they followed his tracks, it became clear he had turned and had stopped running in a haphazard fashion. It seemed he'd set his sights on a target. The *migolmigolo* was circling back to the temporary basecamp, back to where the people—his tormentors—were. Before the day was out, he had planned on staying true to his name. He sought to wear the crown of the widow-maker.

The blood trail ran in a perfectly straight line now, and a chill ran down Charles's spine. The bull didn't even try to hide. He *knew* where he was heading. Over the years, hunters had taught Charles that the African buffalo has poor sight and hearing, so he relies on his ability to smell. But this *migolomigolo* had good ears as well. He must have heard the hunting party moving around in the bush.

It was difficult to believe these *Amissioni* had ever been on a hunt. They broke all the rules, even the cardinal one: maintaining silence. To crown their inexperience, they misbehaved like delinquent teenagers on a school ground.

"Chombe, can we go *faster?*" Phil had caught up from behind, breathing hard. "The *njati* is heading straight to the camp!"

"I see that!" Charles said.

The men broke into a jog.

"They only have two rifles between them," Phil said, puffing. "Will it help if we fire a warning shot?"

"That may make them drop their guard," Louis said.

"They'll think we got him this time," Charles added.

Charles slowed down. The horizon's yellow faded into a pale rose. They had fifteen minutes of light remaining.

It was impossible to see holes, ruts, snakes, or rocks as they ambled forward. They couldn't be too far. Pemba was better than Charles with keeping on a spoor and knowing exactly where he was at all times.

"How far, Chombe?" Louis sounded winded.

"Close," Charles whispered and held up his hand, then stopped. "Listen."

They all paused and caught their breaths again. Around them, the bush prepared for the night. Birds flocked back into the trees, their incessant calling only overshadowed by the tireless cicadas.

"Come." Charles moved forward, his finger on his lips. He pointed to their right. The blood spatter was more difficult to discern now. The blood and the shadows had the same appearance. The bull was smart—he stuck to the bush—and would not dare come into the open. They had reached the edge of the tree line. Ahead of them stretched a narrow plain, across which lay the clusters of trees marking the temporary camp. Charles lowered his binoculars and edged them on.

They took a shortcut across the plain. It would take too long to stick to the tree line. He was certain he'd seen movement in a dense cluster of trees to their far right, about four hundred yards from the camp.

He raised his hand, then beckoned the men closer. "The bull is among those trees." He pointed until they nodded.

The men studied the trees through their binoculars.

"*Bwana* Ferreira, what do you think? Shall we spread out and come around him? Make certain he can't escape? But close enough so we can see each other and not shoot by mistake? *Inde?*"

"Yes, let's go," Louis whispered. Phil gave a thumbs-up. This bull could hear from miles away it seemed.

The rose-painted sky above the horizon was fast turning gray.

They were a hundred yards from the cluster of trees. They had to get much closer in the poor light. There was no room for another mistake.

Through the trees to their left were the telltale signs of a campfire throwing golden shadows into the night.

Sixty yards from the cluster.

They kept their semicircle. Charles raised his arm and waved his hand: forward.

Fifty yards.

Charles's hand shot up. The men froze.

His hand winked. Forward.

Forty yards.

Trees, shrubs, shadows and beast had all become one.

One shadow moved.

It charged. It was fast.

Thirty yards.

Charles could hear the bull's snorting and gasping breaths as he stormed closer.

"*Jesu*! Shoot!"

Three shots rang out. The bull lurched, stumbled, then swerved and took off, uncertain on his feet.

"Reload!" Charles cussed as he struggled to get another round into the chamber.

Phil hollered at the top of his lungs. "Ulrich! He's coming your way!"

Louis had joined them. "He's a bloody *mzimu*! He's a ghost. He won't die!"

The trio raced after the dark form of the beast as he stormed into the early evening, toward the camp where the fire was blazing, zeroing in like a kamikaze pilot, preparing for his final performance.

Charles shouted in *Chinyanja* at Pemba as they darted toward the line of trees with the glow of the fire beyond it. They could see people moving by the fire.

"Rianna! Watch out!" Phil yelled as he rounded the bushes, coming into the clearing.

"Daddy!"

A shot rang out. And another.

Rianna shrieked.

Pemba's voice cut through the night. *"Jesu Christu!"*

## 11

## *Sending for help in the bush*

The *migolomigolo* had stopped grunting. He lay halfway on top of Pemba. Neither of them moved. Whether the bull had sensed the whereabouts of the man who had broken two sticks on his snout was never established. As two more bullets slugged into his colossal body, he still managed to gore the slim *Chichewa* man where he had been standing next to the fire. It was an eye for an eye.

Rianna scampered to her knees and then to her feet to get away from the carcass and the tracker, only to topple on her side. She cried as her leg failed to carry her weight.

"Daddy!"

Phil lurched forward and dragged her to safety. She sobbed with halting breaths, clinging to him. She was next to Pemba when the buffalo had burst onto the scene. Their momentum had knocked her headfirst into the dirt and snapped her leg.

"Can't breathe . . . hurts . . . every time."

"Let me see," Phil said.

Her left leg lay at an awkward angle. Like the tracker, she was covered with dirt and blood. She pulled her now-torn shirt sideways and up over her lower ribs for him to see.

Phil knelt next to his daughter in the dirt. They were fifteen feet away from the blazing fire.

The other men ran over to help free Pemba.

"Daddy . . . feel . . . here." Her breaths were staccato.

An abrasion the size of a man's fanned fingers covered her lower chest. With each breath, a part of her chest the size of a tennis ball pulled inward. The training bra was pushed upward, exposing her budding pubescent breast, the nipple and areola pink-brown in the glare of the fire.

"I'm thirsty." Rianna whimpered.

Phil pulled her shirt down—his own breathing came fast. *You are so much like your mother. Tough. Several of the ribs on the right must be broken. Her leg needs a splint. What about Pemba?* He spun around as the men pulled the tracker free. *Dear Lord, both of them need a hospital! What have we done?*

———

Louis and Ulrich assisted Charles as he carried Pemba's broken body closer to the heat and light of the fire. They made a make-shift stretcher from a sleeping bag and stuffed a rolled bush jacket under his head. Pemba's blood was everywhere and on every-thing—or was it the buffalo's?

Blood trickled from Pemba's nose and mouth. Gargling sounds escaped his throat. The bull had ripped him open from his belly button to below his right nipple. How it missed his liver was a miracle. Pemba couldn't speak. With each jagged breath, his right lung popped out like a pink balloon between shattered ribs.

Kobus ran to get the backpack with the medical supplies.

Charles wept as he knelt next to his friend, covered the wound with his handkerchief, then plopped down and put Pemba's head in his lap. He wiped his mouth clean from blood, murmuring encouragement in *Chinyanja*. One needed no medical degree to tell the tracker was fighting for his life.

Charles swayed back and forth as he mumbled incoherently. His muscled shoulders shook like that of a young boy, sobbing in silence.

Ulrich ran and stoked the fire, anything to keep his trem-bling hands occupied. They needed light.

"We need to get *both* of them to a doctor!" Phil yelled as he ran over to where Louis tended to Pemba.

Kobus had laid the scant items open on a canvas roll next to the fire and Pemba: bandages, gauze, a roll of plaster, a pair of scissors, alcohol in a small bottle, a triangular bandage, aspirins, mercurochrome, and a bottle of malaria pills. It was clear to any layperson that old Dr. Brown would have to be spoken to. The inventory had to be expanded.

Louis glanced at Phil, the station maintenance man. "Thank you for the opinion, *Dr. Vermeulen*." He motioned in Rianna's direction. "What's wrong with *her*?"

Phil balled his fists.

"*Her* has broken ribs and a broken left leg." Phil dropped down next to Kobus. He ignored Louis. "I need a bandage to splint her leg. *Anybody* have a knife? I'll cut a few straight pieces from a branch."

"Here's a knife, Phil" Ulrich held out his hand as sweat dripped from him. He glowed. The fire he'd built could smelter iron ore.

Louis jumped to his feet and scrambled around, searching through the satchels. "People, I need a piece of plastic!" He glanced at the men. The fire's amber tongues cast flickering shadows over them all.

"What do you need the plastic for, *Dr. Ferreira*?" Phil asked as he cut a branch clean.

Louis spun toward his friend, his face drawn. He took five deep breaths because that's what Maria had told him to do.

"It will help his breathing if we can *seal* the wound—push the lung back. It's sucking too much air."

Louis turned to Ulrich. "Please grind three aspirins to powder and make it into a watery paste—a suspension. We don't have morphine."

He glanced at Charles. "Can you make him drink that?"

Rianna had crawled on her hands and knees till she reached Charles and Pemba.

"Rianna! Your leg! Be *careful!*" Phil hollered. As he stepped closer, he snapped the cut branch in two and cut the edges clean.

"Daddy . . . please . . . let me help Charles."

Ulrich waved a small piece of canvas. "How about *this* Louis? It's thin and clean. Wipe it with alcohol and tape it in place with the plaster?"

The men set to work.

Once Phil splinted her leg, Rianna, refusing to back down, assisted Charles in dribbling the aspirin suspension past Pemba's lips.

Rianna received two aspirins and water.

Pemba slipped in and out of consciousness. They splinted his right arm fracture and covered the long wound in its entirety. It seemed that the piece of canvas was helping his breathing—the leak was smaller. His pulse remained weak.

Phil paced next to the fire. "Who knows how to get to the Luwi Bush Camp?"

The fire snapped and crackled, sending bursts of gold specks into the night sky. The faces around the fire stared at him, all transfixed by the fire and the day's events.

A hyena barked in the distance. They must have smelled the dead buffalo.

"Rianna needs a doctor—her ribs," Phil said.

"What about *Pemba*?" Louis asked.

"He's *dying*. She's young, she still has—"

"He's *just* as important as your—"

"He's a professional. He knew what he was letting himself in for!" Phil mumbled.

"*Bwanas*! I'll go." Charles had wiggled himself free from his bloodied friend and wiped his hands clean. He towered next to the fire. "I know where the Luwi Camp is." He glanced at the *Amissioni*.

Phil and Louis both stepped forward, glaring at one another. "I'll come with you," they both said.

Everyone laughed.

Charles shook his head. His face was grim. "*Zikomo, bwanas.* I only need *one*. If we run, we can be at Luwi in thirty minutes, by half past seven. I have one flashlight."

Phil took another step forward.

Louis took his arm. Phil ripped his arm free.

"*Phil!* Let *me* go. The buffalo's dead. *I* must do this . . . It's because of me—" Louis wiped over his eyes and pointed to the buffalo and Pemba and Rianna. His stooped figure made him look ninety.

The two missionaries sized one another.

"*Bwana. Come.*" Charles knelt down and cradled Pemba, careful not to crush anything. "Goodbye, my friend," he whispered.

He snapped to his feet when the heckling laugh of a hyena followed that of a second hyena's bark. The animals were close now, perhaps only outside the glow of the fire. The equivalent of the African drumbeat had sent its message into the night, to the animal kingdom: A king of the forest has fallen. There's a scavenge to scour. There's a feast to be had.

Ulrich, Louis, and Phil broke out of their trance and dragged a fallen tree closer, then heaved it into the fire.

"Kobus!" Louis called. "Keep your rifle ready! Safety off. Those night crawlers can barge in at any moment!" He faced the other men. "Grab *every* dry branch you can find! The *fisis* are here!" He dragged another piece of wood closer. "The hyenas don't like a *bonfire!*"

---

The flashlight's beam paled in comparison to the light of the fire Charles and Louis had stepped away from. They had helped the others build a fire the size of a two-story building. Half the Luangwa valley was now lit. The cackle of hyenas had grown in volume. Scores of glowing eyes darted around them in the darkness. The two men walked side-by-side, almost touching at the hip, their rifles pointing outward, fingers on the triggers.

Charles had once watched as ten of the spotted scavengers had killed a grown lion who'd dared to wander from the pride. *The hyenas must smell the blood of the bull and Pemba on us.* There was no water to wash before they left. The larger its pack, the braver the *fisis* became.

Once they had the fire a hundred yards behind them, Charles glanced at the early night sky. Not many stars were out. "Pemba said we should go east." He aimed with his flashlight hand; the other held his rifle.

The two men had just set off at a steady pace, jogging side-by-side, when a voice hollered behind them, "Louis! Charles! Wait!"

They spun around, sending gravel flying, peering into the path they'd just left. A faint glare of the fire was still visible between the trees. Phil Vermeulen appeared out of the shadows, rifle in his hands, breathing hard.

"Phil, what the *hell*?"

"I'm coming *with* you."

Louis grabbed the flashlight form Charles and shone it on Phil's face. "Have you lost your mind? Your daughter is seriously injured. Our tracker is dying. The hyenas have surrounded—"

"Pemba will die anyways. Rianna's fine. I can't do anything more for her—"

Louis charged at his friend, aiming to strike him with the torch. "You *bastard*!"

"*Bwanas!*"

A hyena barked mere feet away. Charles pulled his rifle into his shoulder and fired at the shapeless form rushing at them. The animal yelped. They heard the plop as he fell and rolled into the dirt. It was too dark to see much. His fellow spotted friends scurried away as Louis brandished the light like a saber in front of him, catching glimpses of hind legs disappearing into the darkness.

Louis ran toward the slumped animal, the flashlight pointing. "Charles, keep your rifle on him!"

He gave the carcass a kick. "He's dead. Good shot, Chombe!"

Then he turned back to Vermeulen, tapping him on the chest. "Do you want more people killed tonight? He handed the light back to Charles and wiped over his face. The anger had left his voice. "Please, Phil . . . Go back. They need you. *Rianna* needs you."

"Louis!" Phil had stepped closer to his friend and grabbed his arm. His voice was a whisper now. "I'm *scared*. What if she *dies*?"

"She'll make it." Louis murmured.

"*Bwanas!* Stop it! *Bwana* Phil, I promise—*Bwana* Louis and I will run fast and hard. Now go back. *Please.*"

The two men spun around and disappeared into the night, heading east.

Phil Vermeulen shuffled back toward the golden glare of the campfire, his finger on the trigger.

———

The two men ran light-footed and held their rifles loosely with their safeties off. Who knew what other night creature had decided to attend the banquet?

The hyenas' heckling grew fainter.

Now was not the time to talk.

Charles tried to spare the batteries. Only when the trees and bush cast too dark a shadow or when safe navigation was impossible over uneven terrain did he use the flashlight.

Each time they required light, they paused and listened before turning on the flashlight. The large predators in the area were on the prowl now and earlier than usual because of the buffalo. And now they'd added a *fisi* to the menu. A more pressing concern were members of the cat family. Lions were less vocal than the hyenas. It seemed the animals had lost their fear of man.

They were halfway to the Number 5 road when they heard the first *umph* of a lion. They froze and listened.

Charles turned to his companion as they ran. "Why is that you and *Bwana* Vermeulen cannot tolerate each other?" His breathing came fast, as did Louis's.

Louis shrugged his shoulders. "Incompatible personalities."

Charles snorted. "*Bwana*? I'm not a child."

"We had a fallout three years ago. Vermeulen is a difficult man."

Charles snickered.

"My wife convinced me to make peace. We did. We became good friends."

Charles beamed the light ahead as they passed through an ominous spot. *"Friends?"* He chuckled. "The *Amissioni* are trying to convert us, the *Chinyanjas*. Perhaps *we* must teach *you* what true friendship is. Teach *you* about brotherly love."

Louis shrugged. "Perhaps," he panted. "This hunt was intended to be a celebration, a highlight of our friendship."

"You act like enemies."

"His daughter was not supposed to have come along."

*"Bwana."* The tall *Chinyanja* tried to catch his breath. "She is only a *mtsikana*. A very clever young girl. Don't blame *her*."

Louis remained silent.

"You know what the *Chinyanjas* call her?"

Louis scoffed. "The girl in the mango tree?"

*"Inde!"* Charles laughed as he pointed the light at their feet.

"You talked about the AB and the old *bwana* in Lusaka. I think *that* is the *true* reason, no?"

Louis's face was drawn. "No. You don't know what you're talking about." He glanced sideways at the African as they navigated the veld. "I can't expect you to understand all of this. You're only a house boy."

Charles scowled at the white missionary as they ran ahead in the night.

Silence was a better answer.

"I read, *bwana*. I listen. I think. I don't need the professor to tell me how to think with my heart. Some days I wonder if your people, the *Amissioni* who came from the South, are any better than the *mzungu*, the white people who came from the North. The Queen and her people stole our land. The *Amissioni*, it seems, stole our hearts."

"Charles?"

"*Inde, bwana*. It's about the AB. That's why Vermeulen hates you. And you do so in return."

Louis stopped running, forcing his companion to do likewise. "I don't *hate* him."

"You don't show that you care for him."

They paused, chucked some water down, leaned forward, and rested their hands on their knees before taking off again.

"My people are different from yours, Charles."

"I have a black skin, *bwana*. I am always reminded of that."

"That's not what I'm *talking* about! The Afrikaners do things different from the *Chichewas*. We do not think the same, about *many* things . . . And, more important, life's not a joke. It's dead serious. We busy ourselves with so many things that have no eternal value."

"You're wrong, *bwana*. Respect and love for my brother do not ask the color of my skin or the language that I speak. It's about my heart. How much light or darkness there is inside . . . *That* has eternal value. Not doctrine."

Louis laughed. "You sound like a *mbusa* now!"

Charles smiled. *A pastor?* He said nothing. *The* mzungu *from the South think they know everything. This* mbusa *has much to learn.*

They ran farther in silence.

"Will you teach me about the Afrikaner *Broederbond, bwana*?"

Louis laughed as if embarrassed.

"We have time, *bwana*. We're almost at the road. I told you: Charles listens well."

Louis told the tall *Chinyanja* who jogged next to him through the African bush about the secret organization that was born a few short years following the First World War. He told him how the AB had sprouted from the conviction that the Afrikaner people had been planted in the country through divine intervention.

They were not far from the gravel road now. Louis thought he'd heard a vehicle ramble past. They had to cross a short dark valley to get to the road.

Louis stopped talking as he grabbed his partner's arm and made him halt. He checked his safety. *There it is again. The umph of a big cat. Then another umph. Is there more than one?*

"*Mkango*," Charles murmured.

The men crouched, their backs toward each other. Leaves rustled. Louis jumped when he stepped on a twig and it snapped. It was as loud as a fired gun.

"*Bwana!*" Charles's warning was mixed with a bone-chilling roar as he fired his rifle. Louis's rifle was knocked from his hands as Charles's spinning figure threw him off balance. Perhaps it had also saved his life from the maned lion who pounced upon him, sending him crashing into the underbrush.

Charles crawled on all fours for Louis's rifle. There was no time to reload. He was certain he'd hit the lion. He rolled on his back, the borrowed rifle in his hands. The male lion bit into Louis's calf and dragged him from under the bush, which had provided momentary protection. Louis's screams cut through the night.

Charles aimed this time. *How will I explain to the police officer why I shot the Amissioni, arrogant and misled as he was?* He pulled the trigger.

The lion let go of the leg and stumbled sideways. He gave a feeble roar, dropped his head, and lurched toward Charles.

Charles scrambled to his feet, lost his footing, and tumbled backward, away from the animal, screaming in *Chinyanja*, still trying to push a round in the chamber. He hollered in agony as the beast's jaw closed around his leg, just above his boot. He jabbed the lion in the face on his snout, with the base of the rifle, smashing his nose. The lion roared as he backed off for a second.

A single shot rang out. The lion toppled on his side. Louis Ferreira stood fifteen feet away, swaying on uncertain legs, rifle in his shoulder.

"*Charles*, are you okay?" Louis hobbled over, using the rifle as a cane, pressing the butt on the ground. He laughed and cried as he fumbled and pushed another round in place. *Who knows how many beasts are still around?*

"I *got* the bastard!"

The *Amissioni* and the *Chinyanja* reached the Luwi Bush Camp fifteen minutes later. They held on to each other with their rifles as canes as they shuffled down the gravel road. Both had torn shirts on. The sleeves had been ripped off to use as emergency bandages for the wounds in their legs and Louis's arm.

———

There was a telephone at the Luwi Bush Camp. Louis alerted the hospital in Fort Jameson and asked them to send an ambulance with a doctor and a nurse—if possible.

He pleaded his case before the camp superintendent to get a vehicle to the injured at the bonfire camp. It didn't require much to commandeer their four-wheel-drive Land Rover.

Then he phoned Maria. She listened without interrupting. She was a wise woman. He also phoned Anna, Phil's spouse and Rianna's mother. He felt little shame as he wept over the phone.

Charles was unmarried and used the time the *bwana* was phoning to get his wounds disinfected and bandaged. He then helped the camp staff load the vehicle with food, water, and a wider variety of emergency medical supplies to apply to the injured in the bush. Anything would help until the doctor could get to them.

The Land Rover was equipped with two spotlights, each the size of a cantaloupe, attached to the roof rack at the front. The 4x4 was built to drive through the African bush.

———

The Luwi Camp Land Rover reached the bonfire camp between the *mopanis* by nine that evening. It was easy to follow the yellow glare between the trees. There was a strong possibility that if a man were standing on the moon, he would see the campfire spectacle in the Luangwa National Park. The *Amissioni* had used each piece of dry wood within a hundred-yard radius for the fire.

Two hyena carcasses lay on the outskirts of the camp. That made three dead hyenas.

The vehicle had not come to a full standstill when Charles swung the rear side door open and hobbled over to the fire. He dropped down next to his friend, took his wrist, and watched his face.

"Pemba."

Pemba didn't answer. His chest had stopped moving by the time Phil had shot the second hyena. Ulrich had shot the first one.

Pemba's hand still felt warm. He'd been lying next to the fire all along.

The flames painted the slim tracker's quiet face with traces of life. They danced over him in the richest warmest colors.

# 12

## *Being good*

The doctor tended to the injured at the Luwi Bush Camp. He saw to it that Charles's and Louis's wounds were disinfected a second time before he sutured them at the hospital, but only after he'd taken care of Rianna. He then wrote the death certificate for Pemba Chiluba

Rianna was admitted to the hospital in Fort Jameson. The doctor couldn't say enough about how impressed he was with the *mopani*-made, four-stick splint that her father had applied as a makeshift stabilizer.

He gave her a pain injection in her bottom, which almost made her cry, more from embarrassment than from pain. The doctor had seen her bare behind!

Rianna was convinced he'd tried to distract her with all his stories while he took an X-ray of her chest, developed it, and then placed a special drainage tube in her chest to help her lung expand better. That was really uncomfortable. At least he had frozen the skin and the tissue between the ribs. She grasped her mother's hand, who by that time had joined them.

Her entire leg was placed in a white plaster cast—another source of embarrassment for the young lady. Cotton was rolled up high onto her thigh, and no one, other than herself, was allowed to touch the inside of her leg!

The plaster of paris felt heavy and warm in the beginning as it set. The pair of crutches made up for everything—and the pampering by the hospital staff. At least she got to eat different stuff than at home!

On the second day, Charles Chombe paid her a visit in hospital. He wore a pair of pants that hid his leg wound. He walked with a subtle limp, the only telltale sign of the ordeal.

He sat down next to her bed.

She took the big man's hand and held it. They sat in silence at first. Then they talked about tracking and about what to look for when deciding the age of a spoor.

Her eyes filled up. "I am so sorry about your friend . . . about Pemba."

Charles sighed.

"It is wrong, Charles . . . wrong that someone gets killed for a silly trophy!"

"He knew it was a dangerous job."

"It's plain wrong!"

"He loved the veld . . . tracking the animals . . . He was not interested in killing them. It was more the challenge of finding them, playing cat and mouse, outwitting them."

"We should make hunting *illegal!*"

Charles laughed. "Do that—when you become president."

"Oh, I will, Mr. Chombe!"

She went home on the fourth day, but only after the doctor was satisfied that her lung had been sufficiently expanded to remove the underwater drainage tube.

———

Three days after Pemba's funeral, Louis Ferreira visited Katete.

Rianna had been back home from the hospital and hopping around with her cast for several days. Her biggest regret was that she had to abstain from climbing her beloved mango tree for six more weeks!

Maria refused to accompany Louis. She said he had to be a man and go make peace without her presence and interference. This time she didn't threaten to take the boys and journey back to her parents in the South. But he still had to go. She told him many things: how much she loved him, but also how important it was for him to get off the mountain—and stay off, for goodness' sake! There was no place in Missions for arrogance. He had to stop striving to live a perfect and righteous life, but instead learn compassion.

"Less doctrine and more compassion, Louis."

———

Phil's wife, Anna, opened the front door.

Louis hesitated.

She leaned forward, pulled him closer, and kissed him on the lips. "Come in, Louis."

"Is Phillip here?" His cheeks glowed.

She laughed. "They're outside, at the back—under the trees. We're having tea."

"Uncle Louis! Look!" Rianna showed off how fast she could cover ground as she hopped closer on her crutches.

"*Bwana*, Ferreira!" Phil held Louis's hand but received a poke from Anna in the ribs.

Louis replied, "Hello, Phil."

They talked about everything—except about why he was there.

"I want you to have the trophy, the head with those majestic horns," Louis said.

"I don't care for it," Phil said. Anna jabbed him in the side a second time—harder this time.

"Well, I don't want to see Pemba every time I walk past it," Louis said.

"You think I don't have nightmares about him gargling in his own blood?"

"Phil!" Anna took his hand and squeezed it.

They all fell quiet.

Louis had closed his eyes. When he looked up, he noticed Rianna hovering. He glanced at Phil and Anna. "Shouldn't she rather go inside while we talk about all this?"

"Do you forget that she stood next to Pemba when the beast gored him and then knocked her to the ground? She saw everything. She heard everything."

Phil jumped up and paced. "When will we stop with the farce, Louis?"

"She's a child."

"Stop the bullshit, Ferreira!"

"Phil!" Anna got up and pulled Phil against her.

Phil spoke. "What example do you think we set for her and Charles that night? We're the missionaries!"

"I know. That's why I came."

"Why *did* you come?" Phil asked.

"I want us to be friends again."

"You can't buy friendship." Phil received a third jab in the ribs.

Louis replied. "I'm not here to buy your goodwill, but I can't live with this on my conscience. I've been so arrogant. So selfish. I believe I need to get the broomstick from my behind."

"Whoa, Louis. Perhaps Rianna *should* go inside."

Rianna giggled. "Daddy, I'm not a baby anymore."

Louis glanced from the daughter to her parents. He jumped up. "No. Please stay, Rianna. You're right. You're a beautiful young lady, who almost got killed . . ." His voice trailed off. He wiped over his eyes. "Pemba wasn't so lucky. A preventable death. And I'm responsible for—"

Louis became unable to speak and plopped down into the chair. He bent forward and clutched his knees. His shoulders shook as he wept.

He looked up, wiped his nose with the back of his hand, and sniffed loudly. "That's why I came . . . I feel responsible for his death."

"Uncle Louis, don't cry. When Charles came to visit me in the hospital, we talked about this. He said Pemba knew how dangerous a job he was doing."

"No, *I'm* responsible."

Phil got up and walked over to his friend, touching his shoulder. "I've got news for you, Ferreira—we *both* carry this burden!"

Louis gawked at his friend.

"Yes, I'm equally hardheaded. I'll come *with* you when you visit Pemba's widow."

"I still can't believe it. That bull had five three-seventy-fives in his body: three through his heart and chest and he wouldn't die. He kept running. He was a *mzimu* . . . a ghost."

Phil grinned. "No, Ferreira. He kept running because I'm as poor a marksman as you are!"

"No, Daddy! It's because he was a *migolomigolo*!"

Be Good - Translation appendix:

*Amissioni* – missionaries
*Amayi* – the madam, the missus, the lady of the household
*Bwalo boy* – gardener, a person of lesser importance
*Broederbond* – Brotherhood
*Bwana* – mister, sir
*Chinyanja* – local language spoken in Zambia. See Chichewa.
*Cooky* – chef, cook, local word for person in charge of the kitchen
*Chadiza* – a town in Eastern Zambia
*Chichewas* – Ethnic African group found in Zambia and Malawi.
They speak Chichewa, also known as Chinyanja or Nyanja
*Chepa* – a little
*Chichira* – hip joint
*Fisi* – hyena
*Grootmense* – adults or grown-ups
*Hubbly-Bubbly* – popular soft drink in Southern Africa during
the 1960s and 1970s
*Inde* – yes, indeed
*Iyayi* – no
*Kleintjies* – the little ones, the young ones
*Katete* – name of one of the Mission stations
*Magwero* – name of a Mission station
*Mwanas* - children
*Madzi Moyo* – name of a Mission station (meaning: water of life)
*Moni, Mbusa* – "Hello, pastor."
*Muli bwanyi* – "How are you?"
*Mopani* – tree found in Southern Africa

*Migolomigolo* – massive, large, gigantic

*Mtsikana* – young girl

*Mtengo* – trees

*Mzimu* – ghost

*Mkango* – lion

*Nditho* – truly

*Njati* – buffalo

*Njanji* – tracks

*Oubaas* – The Boss, the old man, an older male

*"Pappie 'seblief"* – "Daddy please."

*Spoor* – tracks; the trail, droppings, scent, or telltale signs of an animal

*Veld* – grassland, bush, field, African savannah

*Witbroodjie* – favorite

*Wamasiye wolenga* – the widow-maker

*Wosaka* – hunter

*Wakuda kufa* – Black death

*Zikuyenda* – "What's the problem? What's wrong? What's up?"

*Zikomo* – "Thank you."

*Zikomo kwambiri* – "Thank you very much!"

www.ingramcontent.com/pod-product-compliance
Lightning Source LLC
Chambersburg PA
CBHW030547130626
46552CB00006B/2472